MEE   N

Fafhr   ross
the two   senseless. Each discerned
something inexplicably familiar in the other.

Fafhrd said, "Our motives for being here seem identical."

"Seem? Surely must be!" the Mouser answered curtly.

"You said?"

"I said, 'Seem? Surely must be!' "

"How civilized of you!" Fafhrd commented in pleased tones.

"Civilized?" the Mouser demanded suspiciously, gripping his dirk tighter.

"To care, in the eye of action, exactly what's said," Fafhrd explained. Without letting the Mouser out of his vision, he glanced down. His gaze traveled from the belt and pouch of one fallen thief to those of the other. Then he looked up at the Mouser with a broad, ingenuous smile.

"Sixty-sixty?" he suggested.

FRITZ LEIBER

ILL MET IN LANKHMAR

TOR
fantasy

A TOM DOHERTY ASSOCIATES BOOK
NEW YORK

ILL MET IN LANKHMAR

Copyright © 1969, 1970 by Mercury Press, Inc.; copyright © 1970 by Fritz Leiber

A Tor Book
Published by Tom Doherty Associates, Inc.
49 West 24th Street
New York, N.Y. 10010

Cover art © 1989 by Sam Rakeland

ISBN: 0-812-50821-1   Can. ISBN: 0-812-50820-3

First Tor edition: March 1990

Printed in the United States of America

0 9 8 7 6 5 4 3 2 1

Silent as specters, the tall and the fat thief edged past the dead, noose-strangled watch-leopard, out the thick, lock-picked door of Jengao the Gem Merchant, and strolled east on Cash Street through the thin black night-smog of Lankhmar, City of Sevenscore Thousand Smokes.

East on Cash it had to be, for west at the intersection of Cash and Silver was a police post with unbribed guardsmen in browned-iron cuirasses and helms, restlessly grounding and rattling their pikes, while Jengao's place had no alley entrance or even window in its stone walls three spans thick and the roof and floor almost as strong and without trapdoors.

1

But tall, tight-lipped Slevyas, master thief candidate, and fat, darting-eyed Fissif, thief second class, brevetted first class for this operation, with a rating of talented in double-dealing, were not in the least worried. Everything was proceeding according to plan. Each carried thonged in his pouch a much smaller pouch of jewels of the first water only, for Jengao, now breathing stentoriously inside and senseless from the slugging he'd suffered, must be allowed, nay, nursed and encouraged, to build up his business again and so ripen it for another plucking. Almost the first law of the Thieves' Guild was never kill the hen that laid brown eggs with a ruby in the yolk, or white eggs with a diamond in the white.

The two thieves also had the relief of knowing that, with the satisfaction of a job well done, they were going straight home now, not to a wife, Aarth forbid!—or to parents and children, all gods forfend!—but to Thieves' House, headquarters and barracks of the all-mighty Guild which was father to them both and mother too, though no woman was allowed inside its ever-open portal on Cheap Street.

In addition there was the comforting knowledge that although each was armed only with his regulation silver-hilted thief's knife, a weapon seldom used except in rare intramural duels and brawls, in fact more a membership token than a weapon, they were nevertheless most strongly convoyed by three reliable and lethal bravos hired for the evening from the Slayers' Brotherhood, one moving well ahead of them as point, the other two well behind as rear guard and chief striking force, in fact almost out of sight—for it is never wise that such convoying be obvious, or so believed Krovas, Grandmaster of the Thieves' Guild.

And if all that were not enough to make Slevyas and Fissif feel safe and serene, there danced along soundlessly beside them in the shadow of the north curb a small, malformed or at any rate somewhat large-headed shape that might have been a small dog, a somewhat undersized cat, or a very big rat. Occasionally it scuttled familiarly and even encouragingly a little way toward their snugly felt-slippered feet, though it always scurried swiftly back into the darker dark.

True, this last guard was not an absolutely unalloyed reassurance. At that very moment, scarcely twoscore paces yet from Jengao's, Fissif tautly walked for a bit on tiptoe and strained his pudgy lips upward to whisper softly in Slevyas' long-lobed ear, "Damned if I like being dogged by that Familiar of Hristomilo, no matter what security he's supposed to afford us. Bad enough that Krovas employs or lets himself be cowed into employing a sorcerer of most

3

dubious, if dire, reputation and aspect, but that—"

"Shut your trap!" Slevyas hissed still more softly.

Fissif obeyed with a shrug and occupied himself even more restlessly and keenly than was his wont in darting his gaze this way and that, but chiefly ahead.

Some distance in that direction, in fact just short of the Gold Street intersection, Cash was bridged by an enclosed second-story passageway connecting the two buildings which made up the premises of the famous stone-masons and sculptors Rokkermas and Slaarg. The firm's buildings themselves were fronted by very shallow porticos supported by unnecessarily large pillars of varied shape and decoration, advertisements more than structural members.

From just beyond the bridge there came two low, brief whistles, signal from the point bravo that he had inspected that area for ambushes and discovered nothing suspicious and that Gold Street was clear.

Fissif was by no means entirely satisfied by the safety signal. To tell the truth, the fat thief rather enjoyed being apprehensive and even fearful, at least up to a point. A sense of strident panic overlaid with writhing calm made him feel more excitingly alive than the occasional woman he enjoyed. So he scanned most closely through

4

the thin, sooty smog the frontages and over-
hangs of Rokkermas and Slaarg as his and
Slevyas' leisurely seeming yet unslow pace
brought them steadily closer.

On this side the bridge was pierced by
four small windows, between which were
three large niches in which stood—another
advertisement—three life-size plaster statues, somewhat eroded by years of weather
and dyed varyingly tones of dark gray by as
many years of smog. Approaching Jengao's
before the burglary, Fissif had noted them
with a swift but comprehensive over-
shoulder glance. Now it seemed to him that
the statue to the right had indefinably
changed. It was that of a man of medium
height wearing cloak and hood, who gazed
down with crossed arms and brooding aspect. No, not indefinably quite—the statue
was a more uniform dark gray now, he fan-
cied, cloak, hood, and face; it seemed somewhat sharper featured, less eroded; and he
would almost swear it had grown shorter!

Just below the niche, moreover, there was
in the street a scattering of gray and raw
white rubble which he didn't recall having
been there earlier. He strained to remember if during the excitement of the burglary, with its lively leopard-slaying and
slugging and all, the unsleeping watch-
corner of his mind had recorded a distant
crash, and now he believed it had. His quick
imagination pictured the possibility of a

hole or even door behind each statue, through which it might be given a strong push and so tumbled onto passersby, himself and Slevyas specifically, the right-hand statue having been crashed to test the device and then replaced with a near twin.

He would keep close watch on all three statues as he and Slevyas walked under. It would be easy to dodge if he saw one start to overbalance. Should he yank Slevyas out of harm's way when that happened? It was something to think about.

Without pause his restless attention fixed next on the porticos and pillars. The latter, thick and almost three yards tall, were placed at irregular intervals as well as being irregularly shaped and fluted, for Rokkermas and Slaarg were most modern and emphasized the unfinished look, randomness, and the unexpected.

Nevertheless it seemed to Fissif, his wariness wide awake now, that there was an intensification of unexpectedness, specifically that there was one more pillar under the porticos than when he had last passed by. He couldn't be sure which pillar was the newcomer, but he was almost certain there was one.

Share his suspicions with Slevyas? Yes, and get another hissed reproof and flash of contempt from the small, dull-seeming eyes.

The enclosed bridge was close now. Fissif glanced up at the right-hand statue and noted other differences from the one he'd recalled. Although shorter, it seemed to hold itself more strainingly erect, while the frown carved in its dark gray face was not so much one of philosophic brooding as sneering contempt, self-conscious cleverness, and conceit.

Still, none of the three statues toppled forward as he and Slevyas walked under the bridge. However, something else happened to Fissif at that moment.

One of the pillars winked at him.

The Gray Mouser—for so Mouse now named himself to himself and his beloved Ivrian—turned around in the right-hand niche, leaped up and caught hold of the cornice, silently vaulted to the flat roof, and crossed it precisely in time to see the two thieves emerge below.

Without hesitation he leaped forward and down, his body straight as a crossbow bolt, the soles of his ratskin boots aimed at the shorter thief's fat-buried shoulder blades, though leading him a little to allow for the yard he'd walk while the Mouser hurtled toward him.

In the instant that he leaped, the tall thief glanced up overshoulder and whipped out a knife, though making no move to push or pull Fissif out of the way of the human projectile speeding toward him. The Mouser shrugged in full flight. He'd just have to deal with the tall thief faster after knocking down the fat one.

More swiftly than one would have thought he could manage, Fissif whirled around then and thinly screamed, "Slivikin!"

The ratskin boots took him high in the belly. It was like landing on a big cushion. Writhing aside from Slevyas' first thrust, the Mouser somersaulted forward, turning feet over head, and as the fat thief's skull hit a cobble with a dull *bong* he came to his feet with dirk in hand, ready to take on the tall one.

But there was no need. Slevyas, his small eyes glazed, was toppling too.

One of the pillars had sprung forward, trailing a voluminous robe. A big hood had fallen back from a youthful face and long-haired head. Brawny arms had emerged from the long, loose sleeves that had been the pillar's topmost section, while the big fist ending one of the arms had dealt Slevyas a shrewd knockout punch on the chin.

Fafhrd and the Gray Mouser faced each other across the two thieves sprawled senseless. They were poised for attack, yet for the moment neither moved.

Each discerned something inexplicably familiar in the other.

Fafhrd said, "Our motives for being here seem identical."

"Seem? Surely must be!" the Mouser answered curtly, fiercely eyeing this potential new foe, who was taller by a head than the tall thief.

"You said?"

"I said, 'Seem? Surely must be!'"

"How civilized of you!" Fafhrd commented in pleased tones.

"Civilized?" the Mouser demanded suspiciously, gripping his dirk tighter.

"To care, in the eye of action, exactly what's said," Fafhrd explained. Without letting the Mouser out of his vision, he glanced down. His gaze traveled from the belt and pouch of one fallen thief to those of the other. Then he looked up at the Mouser with a broad, ingenuous smile.

"Sixty-sixty?" he suggested.

The Mouser hesitated, sheathed his dirk, and rapped out, "A deal!" He knelt abruptly, his fingers on the drawstrings of Fissif's pouch. "Loot your Slivikin," he directed.

It was natural to suppose that the fat thief had been crying his companion's name at the end.

Without looking up from where he knelt, Fafhrd remarked, "That . . . ferret they had with them. Where did it go?"

"Ferret?" the Mouser answered briefly. "It was a marmoset!"

"Marmoset," Fafhrd mused. "That's a small tropical monkey, isn't it? Well, might have been, but I got the strange impression that—"

The silent, two-pronged rush which almost overwhelmed them at that instant really surprised neither of them. Each had been expecting it, but the expectation had dropped out of conscious thought with the startlement of their encounter.

The three bravos racing down upon them in concerted attack, two from the west and one from the east, all with swords poised to thrust, had assumed that the two highjackers would be armed at most with knives and as timid or at least cautious in weapons-combat as the general run of thieves and counter-thieves. So it was they who were surprised and thrown into confusion when with the lightning speed of youth the Mouser and Fafhrd sprang up, whipped out fearsomely long swords, and faced them back to back.

The Mouser made a very small parry in carte so that the thrust of the bravo from the east went past his left side by only a hair's breath. He instantly riposted. His adversary, desperately springing back, parried in turn in carte. Hardly slowing, the tip of the Mouser's long, slim sword dropped under that parry with the delicacy of a princess curtsying and then leaped forward and a little upward, the Mouser making an impossibly long-looking lunge for one so small, and went between two scales of the bravo's armored jerkin and between his ribs and through his heart and out his back as if all were angelfood cake.

Meanwhile Fafhrd, facing the two bravos from the west, swept aside their low thrusts with somewhat larger, down-sweeping parries in seconde and low prime, then flipped up his sword, long as the Mouser's but heavier, so that it slashed through the neck of his right-hand adversary, half decapitating him. Then he, dropping back a swift step, readied a thrust for the other.

But there was no need. A narrow ribbon of bloodied steel, followed by a gray glove and arm, flashed past him from behind and transfixed the last bravo with the identical thrust the Mouser had used on the first.

The two young men wiped and sheathed their swords. Fafhrd brushed the palm of his open right hand down his robe and held it out. The Mouser pulled off right-hand gray glove and shook the other's big hand in his sinewy one. Without word exchanged, they knelt and finished looting the two unconscious thieves, securing the small bags of jewels. With an oily towel and then a dry one, the Mouser sketchily wiped from his face the greasy ash-soot mixture which had darkened it, next swiftly rolled up both towels and returned them to his own pouch. Then, after only a questioning eye-twitch east on the Mouser's part and a nod from Fafhrd, they swiftly walked on in the direc-

11

tion Slevyas and Fissif and their escort had been going.

After reconnoitering Gold Street, they crossed it and continued east on Cash at Fafhrd's gestured proposal.

"My woman's at the Golden Lamprey," he explained.

"Let's pick her up and take her home to meet my girl," the Mouser suggested.

"Home?" Fafhrd inquired politely, only the barest hint of question in his voice.

"Dim Lane," the Mouser volunteered.

"Silver Eel?"

"Behind it. We'll have some drinks."

"I'll pick up a jug. Never have too much juice."

"True. I'll let you."

Several squares farther on Fafhrd, after stealing a number of looks at his new comrade, said with conviction, "We've met before."

The Mouser grinned at him. "Beach by the Mountains of Hunger?"

"Right! When I was a pirate's ship-boy."

"And I was a wizard's apprentice."

Fafhrd stopped, again wiped right hand on robe, and held it out. "Name's Fafhrd. Ef ay ef aitch ar dee."

Again the Mouser shook it. "Gray Mouser," he said a touch defiantly, as if challenging anyone to laugh at the sobriquet. "Excuse me, but how exactly do you pronounce that? Faf-hrud?"

12

"Just Faf-erd."

"Thank you." They walked on.

"Gray Mouser, eh?" Fafhrd remarked. "Well, you killed yourself a couple of rats tonight."

"That I did." The Mouser's chest swelled and he threw back his head. Then with a comic twitch of his nose and a sidewise half-grin he admitted, "You'd have got your second man easily enough. I stole him from you to demonstrate my speed. Besides, I was excited."

Fafhrd chuckled. "You're telling me? How do you suppose I was feeling?"

Later, as they were crossing Pimp Street, he asked, "Learn much magic from your wizard?"

Once more the Mouser threw back his head. He flared his nostrils and drew down the corners of his lips, preparing his mouth for boastful, mystifying speech. But once more he found himself twitching his nose and half grinning. What the deuce did this big fellow have that kept him from putting on his usual acts? "Enough to tell me it's damned dangerous stuff. Though I still fool with it now and then."

Fafhrd was asking himself a similar question. All his life he'd mistrusted small men, knowing his height awakened their instant jealousy. But this clever little chap was somehow an exception. Quick thinker and brilliant swordsman too, no argument. He prayed to Kos that Vlana would like him.

On the northeast corner of Cash and Whore a slow-burning torch shaded by a broad gilded hoop cast a cone of light up into the thickening black night-smog and another cone down on the cobbles before the tavern door. Out of the shadows into the second cone stepped Vlana, handsome in a narrow black velvet dress and red stockings, her only ornaments a silver-sheathed and -hilted dagger and a silver-worked black pouch, both on a plain black belt.

Fafhrd introduced the Gray Mouser, who behaved with an almost fawning courtesy, obsequiously gallant. Vlana studied him boldly, then gave him a tentative smile.

Fafhrd opened under the torch the small pouch he'd taken off the tall thief. Vlana looked down into it. She put her arms around Fafhrd, hugged him tight, and kissed him soundly. Then she thrust the jewels into the pouch on her belt.

When that was done, he said, "Look, I'm going to buy a jug. You tell her what happened, Mouser."

When he came out of the Golden Lamprey he was carrying four jugs in the crook of his left arm and wiping his lips on the back of his right hand. Vlana was frowning. He grinned at her. The Mouser smacked his lips at the jugs. They continued east on

Cash. Fafhrd realized that the frown was for more than the jugs and the prospect of stupidly drunken male revelry. The Mouser tactfully walked ahead, ostensibly to lead the way.

When his figure was little more than a blob in the thickening smog, Vlana whispered harshly, "You had two members of the Thieves' Guild knocked out cold and you didn't cut their throats?"

"We slew three bravos," Fafhrd protested by way of excuse.

"My quarrel is not with the Slayers' Brotherhood, but that abominable Guild. You swore to me that whenever you had the chance—"

"Vlana! I couldn't have the Gray Mouser thinking I was an amateur counter-thief consumed by hysteria and blood lust."

"You already set great store by him, don't you?"

"He possibly saved my life tonight."

"Well, he told me that *he'd* have slit their throats in a wink, if he'd known I wanted it that way."

"He was only playing up to you from courtesy."

"Perhaps and perhaps not. But *you* knew and you didn't—"

"Vlana, shut up!"

Her frown became a rageful glare, then suddenly she laughed wildly, smiled twitchingly as if she were about to cry, mastered herself and smiled more lovingly. "Pardon me, darling," she said. "Sometimes you must think I'm going mad and sometimes I believe I am."

"Well, don't," he told her shortly. "Think of the jewels we've won instead. And behave yourself with our new friends. Get some wine inside you and relax. I mean to enjoy myself tonight. I've earned it."

She nodded and clutched his arm in agreement and for comfort and sanity. They hurried to catch up with the dim figure ahead.

The Mouser, turning left, led them a half square north on Cheap Street to where a narrower way went east again. The black mist in it looked solid.

"Dim Lane," the Mouser explained.

Fafhrd nodded that he knew.

Vlana said, "Dim's too weak—too *transparent* a word for it tonight," with an uneven laugh in which there were still traces of hysteria and which ended in a fit of strangled coughing. When she could swallow again, she gasped out, "Damn Lankhmar's night-smog! What a hell of a city!"

"It's the nearness here of the Great Salt Marsh," Fafhrd explained.

And he did indeed have part of the answer. Lying low betwixt the Marsh, the Inner Sea, the River Hlal, and the flat southern grainfields watered by canals fed by the Hlal, Lankhmar with its innumerable smokes was the prey of fogs and sooty smogs. No wonder the citizens had adopted the black toga as their formal garb. Some averred the toga had originally been white or pale brown, but so swiftly soot-blackened, necessitating endless laundering, that a thrifty overlord had ratified and made official what nature or civilization's arts decreed.

About halfway to Carter Street, a tavern on the north side of the lane emerged from the murk. A gape-jawed serpentine shape of pale metal crested with soot hung high for a sign. Beneath it they passed a door curtained with begrimed leather, the slit in which spilled out noise, pulsing torchlight, and the reek of liquor.

Just beyond the Silver Eel the Mouser led them through an inky passageway outside the tavern's east wall. They had to go single file, feeling their way along rough, slimily bemisted brick and keeping close together.

"Mind the puddle," the Mouser warned. "It's deep as the Outer Sea."

The passageway widened. Reflected torchlight filtering down through the dark mist allowed them to make out only the most general shape of their surroundings. To the right was more windowless, high wall. To the left, crowding close to the back of the Silver Eel, rose a dismal, rickety building of darkened brick and blackened, ancient wood. It looked utterly deserted to

Fafhrd and Vlana until they had craned back their heads to gaze at the fourth-story attic under the ragged-guttered roof. There faint lines and points of yellow light shone around and through three tightly-latticed windows. Beyond, crossing the T of the space they were in, was a narrow alley.

"Bones Alley," the Mouser told them in somewhat lofty tones. "I call it Ordure Boulevard."

"I can smell that," Vlana said.

By now she and Fafhrd could see a long, narrow wooden outside stairway, steep yet sagging and without a rail, leading up to the lighted attic. The Mouser relieved Fafhrd of the jugs and went up it quite swiftly.

"Follow me when I've reached the top," he called back. "I think it'll take your weight, Fafhrd, but best one of you at a time."

Fafhrd gently pushed Vlana ahead. With another hysteria-tinged laugh and a pause midway up for another fit of choked coughing, she mounted to the Mouser where he now stood in an open doorway, from which streamed yellow light that died swiftly in the night-smog. He was lightly resting a hand on a big, empty, wrought-iron lamp-hook firmly set in a stone section of the outside wall. He bowed aside, and she went in.

Fafhrd followed, placing his feet as close as he could to the wall, his hands ready to grab for support. The whole stairs creaked ominously and each step gave a little as he shifted his weight onto it. Near the top, one gave way with the muted crack of half-rotted wood. Gently as he could, he sprawled himself hand and knee on as many steps as he could reach, to distribute his weight, and cursed sulphurously.

"Don't fret, the jugs are safe," the Mouser called down gayly.

Fafhrd crawled the rest of the way, a somewhat sour look on his face, and did not get to his feet until he was inside the doorway. When he had done so, he almost gasped with surprise.

It was like rubbing the verdigris from a cheap brass ring and finding a rainbow-fired diamond of the first water set in it. Rich drapes, some twinkling with embroidery of silver and gold, covered the walls except where the shuttered windows were—and the shutters of those were gilded. Similar but darker fabrics hid the low ceiling, making a gorgeous canopy in which the flecks of gold and silver were like stars. Scattered about were plump cushions and low tables, on which burned a multitude of candles. On shelves against the walls were neatly stacked like small logs a vast reserve of candles, numerous scrolls, jugs, bottles, and enameled boxes. A low vanity table was backed by a mirror of honed silver and thickly scattered over with jewels and cosmetics. In a large fireplace was set a small metal stove, neatly blacked, with an ornate fire-pot. Also set beside the stove were a tidy pyramid of thin, resinous torches with frayed ends—fire-kindlers—and other pyramids of short-handled brooms and mops, small, short logs, and gleamingly black coal.

On a low dais by the fireplace was a wide, short-legged, high-backed couch covered with cloth of gold. On it sat a thin, pale-faced, delicately handsome girl clad in a dress of thick violet silk worked with silver and belted with a silver chain. Her slippers were of white snow-serpent fur. Silver pins headed with amethysts held in place her high-piled black hair. Around her shoulders was drawn a white ermine wrap. She was leaning forward with uneasy-seeming graciousness and extending a narrow, white hand which shook a little to Vlana, who knelt before her and now gently took the proffered hand and bowed her head over it, her own glossy, straight, dark-brown hair making a canopy, and pressed the other girl's hand's back to her lips.

Fafhrd was happy to see his woman playing up properly to this definitely odd though delightful situation. Then looking at Vlana's long, red-stockinged leg stretched far behind her as she knelt on the other, he noted that the floor was everywhere strewn—to the point of double, treble, and quadruple overlaps—with thick-piled, close-woven, many-hued rugs of the finest imported from the Eastern Lands. Before he knew it, his thumb had shot toward the Gray Mouser.

"You're the Rug Robber!" he proclaimed. "You're the Carpet Crimp!—and the Candle Corsair too!" he continued, referring to two series of unsolved thefts which had been on the lips of all Lankhmar when he and Vlana had arrived a moon ago.

The Mouser shrugged impassive-faced at Fafhrd, then suddenly grinned, his slitted eyes a-twinkle, and broke into an impromptu dance which carried him whirling and jigging around the room and left him behind Fafhrd, where he deftly reached down the hooded and long-sleeved huge robe from the latter's stooping shoulders, shook it out, carefully folded it, and set it on a pillow.

After a long, uncertain pause, the girl in violet nervously patted with her free hand the cloth of gold beside her and Vlana seated herself there, carefully not too close, and the two women spoke together in low voices, Vlana taking the lead, though not obviously.

The Mouser took off his own gray, hooded cloak, folded it almost fussily, and laid it beside Fafhrd's. Then they unbelted their swords, and the Mouser set them atop folded robe and cloak.

Without those weapons and bulking garments, the two men looked suddenly like youths, both with clear, close-shaven faces, both slender despite the swelling muscles of Fafhrd's arms and calves, he with long red-gold hair falling down his back and about his shoulders, the Mouser with dark hair cut in bangs, the one in brown leather tunic worked with copper wire, the other in jerkin of coarsely woven gray silk.

They smiled at each other. The feeling each had of having turned boy all at once made their smiles for the first time a bit embarrassed. The Mouser cleared his throat and, bowing a little, but looking still at Fafhrd, extended a loosely spread-fingered arm toward the golden couch and said with a preliminary stammer, though otherwise smoothly enough, "Fafhrd, my good friend, permit me to introduce you to my princess. Ivrian, my dear, receive Fafhrd graciously if you please, for tonight he and I fought back to back against three and we conquered."

Fafhrd advanced, stooping a little, the crown of his red-gold hair brushing the be-starred canopy, and knelt before Ivrian exactly as Vlana had. The slender hand extended to him looked steady now, but was still quiveringly a-tremble, he discovered as soon as he touched it. He handled it as if it were silk woven of the white spider's gossamer, barely brushing it with his lips, and still felt nervous as he mumbled some compliments.

He did not sense, at least at the moment, that the Mouser was quite as nervous as he, if not more so, praying hard that Ivrian would not overdo her princess part and snub their guests, or collapse in trembling or tears or run to him or into the next room, for Fafhrd and Vlana were literally the first beings, human or animal, noble, freeman, or slave, that he had brought or allowed into the luxurious nest he had created for his aristocratic beloved—save the two love birds that twittered in a silver cage hanging to the other side of the fireplace from the dais.

Despite his shrewdness and newfound cynicism it never occurred to the Mouser that it was chiefly his charming but preposterous coddling of Ivrian that was keeping doll-like and even making more so the potentially brave and realistic girl who had fled with him from her father's torture chamber four moons ago.

But now as Ivrian smiled at last and Fafhrd gently returned her her hand and cautiously backed off, the Mouser relaxed with relief, fetched two silver cups and two silver mugs, wiped them needlessly with a silken towel, carefully selected a bottle of violet wine, then with a grin at Fafhrd uncorked instead one of the jugs the Northerner had brought, and near-brimmed the

four gleaming vessels and served them all
four.

With another preliminary clearing of
throat, but no trace of stammer this time,
he toasted, "To my greatest theft to date in
Lankhmar, which willy-nilly I must share
sixty-sixty with"—he couldn't resist the
sudden impulse—"with this great, long-
haired, barbarian lout here!" And he
downed a quarter of his mug of pleasantly
burning wine fortified with brandy.

Fafhrd quaffed off half of his, then toasted
back, "To the most boastful and finical little civilized chap I've ever deigned to share
loot with," quaffed off the rest, and with a
great smile that showed white teeth held
out his empty mug.

The Mouser gave him a refill, topped off
his own, then set that down to go to Ivrian
and pour into her lap from their small
pouch the gems he'd filched from Fissif.
They gleamed in their new, enviable loca-
tion like a small puddle of rainbow-hued
quicksilver.

Ivrian jerked back a-tremble, almost
spilling them, but Vlana gently caught her
arm, steadying it, and leaned in over the
jewels with a throaty gasp of wonder and
admiration, slowly turned an envious gaze
on the pale girl, and began rather urgently
but smilingly to whisper to her. Fafhrd realized that Vlana was acting now, but acting well and effectively, since Ivrian was

soon nodding eagerly and not long after that beginning to whisper back. At her direction, Vlana fetched a blue-enameled box inlaid with silver, and the two of them transferred the jewels from Ivrian's lap into its blue velvet interior. Then Ivrian placed the box close beside her and they chatted on.

As he worked through his second mug in smaller gulps, Fafhrd relaxed and began to get a deeper feeling of his surroundings. The dazzling wonder of the first glimpse of this throne room in a slum, its colorful luxury intensified by contrast with the dark and mud and slime and rotten stairs and Ordure Boulevard just outside, faded, and he began to note the ricketiness and rot under the grand overlay.

Black, rotten wood and dry, cracked wood too showed here and there between the drapes and also loosed their sick, ancient stinks. The whole floor sagged under the rugs, as much as a span at the center of the room. A large cockroach was climbing down a gold-worked drape, another toward the couch. Threads of night-smog were coming through the shutters, making evanescent black arabesques against the gilt. The stones of the large fireplace had been scrubbed and varnished, yet most of the mortar was gone from between them; some sagged, others were missing altogether.

The Mouser had been building a fire there

in the stove. Now he pushed in all the way the yellow-flaring kindler he'd lit from the fire-pot, hooked the little black door shut over the mounting flames, and turned back into the room. As if he'd read Fafhrd's mind, he took up several cones of incense, set their peaks a-smolder at the fire-pot, and placed them about the room in gleaming, shallow, brass bowls—stepping hard on the one cockroach by the way and surreptitiously catching and crushing the other in the base of his flicked fist. Then he stuffed silken rags in the widest shutter-cracks, took up his silver mug again, and for a moment gave Fafhrd a very hard look, as if daring him to say just one word against the delightful yet faintly ridiculous doll's house he'd prepared for his princess.

Next moment he was smiling and lifting his mug to Fafhrd, who was doing the same. Need of refills brought them close together. Hardly moving his lips, the Mouser explained sotto voce, "Ivrian's father was a duke. I slew him, by black magic, I believe, while he was having me done to death on the torture rack. A most cruel man, cruel to his daughter too, yet a duke, so that Ivrian is wholly unused to fending or caring for herself. I pride myself that I maintain her in grander state than ever her father did with all his serving men and maids."

Suppressing the instant criticisms he felt of this attitude and program, Fafhrd nodded and said amiably, "Surely you've thieved together a most charming little palace, quite worthy of Lankhmar's overlord Karstak Ovartamortes, or the King of Kings at Tisilinilit."

From the couch Vlana called in her husky contralto, "Gray Mouser, your princess would hear an account of tonight's adventure. And might we have more wine?"

Ivrian called, "Yes, please, Mouse."

Wincing almost imperceptibly at that earlier nickname, the Mouser looked to Fafhrd for the go-ahead, got the nod, and launched into his story. But first he served the girls wine. There wasn't enough for their cups, so he opened another jug and after a moment of thought uncorked all three, setting one by the couch, one by Fafhrd where he sprawled now on the pillowy carpets, and reserving one for himself. Ivrian looked wide-eyed apprehensive at this signal of heavy drinking ahead, Vlana cynical with a touch of anger, but neither voiced their criticism.

The Mouser told the tale of counter-thievery well, acting it out in part, and with only the most artistic of embellishments— the ferret-marmoset before escaping ran up his back and tried to scratch out his eyes— and he was interrupted only twice.

When he said, "And so with a whish and a snick I bared Scalpel—" Fafhrd remarked, "Oh, so you've nicknamed your sword as well as yourself?"

The Mouser drew himself up. "Yes, and I call my dirk Cat's Claw. Any objections? Seems childish to you?"

"Not at all. I call my own sword Graywand. All weapons are in a fashion alive, civilized and nameworthy. Pray continue."

And when he mentioned the beastie of uncertain nature that had gamboled along with the thieves (and attacked his eyes!), Ivrian paled and said with a shudder, "Mouse! That sounds like a witch's familiar!"

"Wizard's," Vlana corrected. "Those gutless Guild-villains have no truck with women, except as fee'd or forced vehicles for their lust. But Krovas, their current king, though superstitious, is noted for taking *all* precautions, and might well have a warlock in his service."

"That seems most likely; it harrows me with dread," the Mouser agreed with ominous gaze and sinister voice. He really didn't believe or feel what he said—he was about as harrowed as virgin prairie—in the least, but he eagerly accepted any and all atmospheric enhancements of his performance.

When he was done, the girls, eyes flashing and fond, toasted him and Fafhrd for their cunning and bravery. The Mouser bowed and eye-twinklingly smiled about, then sprawled him down with a weary sigh, wiping his forehead with a silken cloth and downing a large drink.

After asking Vlana's leave, Fafhrd told the adventurous tale of their escape from Cold Corner—he from his clan, she from an acting troupe—and of their progress to Lankhmar, where they lodged now in an actors' tenement near the Plaza of Dark Delights. Ivrian hugged herself to Vlana and shivered large-eyed at the witchy parts—at least as much in delight as fear of Fafhrd's tale, he thought. He told himself it was natural that a doll-girl should love ghost stories, though he wondered if her pleasure would have been as great if she had known that his ghost stories were truly true. She seemed to live in worlds of imagination—once more at least half the Mouser's doing, he was sure.

The only proper matter he omitted from his account was Vlana's fixed intent to get a monstrous revenge on the Thieves' Guild for torturing to death her accomplices and harrying her out of Lankhmar when she'd tried free-lance thieving in the city, with miming as a cover. Nor of course did he mention his own promise—foolish, he thought now—to help her in this bloody business.

After he'd done and got his applause, he found his throat dry despite his skald's training, but when he sought to wet it, he

discovered that his mug was empty and his
jug too, though he didn't feel in the least
drunk; he had talked all the liquor out of
him, he told himself, a little of the stuff escaping in each glowing word he'd spoken.

The Mouser was in like plight and not
drunk either—though inclined to pause
mysteriously and peer toward infinity before answering question or making remark.
This time he suggested, after a particularly
long infinity-gaze, that Fafhrd accompany
him to the Eel while he purchased a fresh
supply.

"But we've a lot of wine left in *our* jug,"
Ivrian protested. "Or at least a little," she
amended. It did sound empty when Vlana
shook it. "Besides, you've wine of all sorts
here."

"Not this sort, dearest, and first rule is
never mix 'em," the Mouser explained, wag-
ging a finger. "That way lies unhealth, aye,
and madness."

"My dear," Vlana said, sympathetically
patting Ivrian's wrist, "at some time in any
good party all the men who are really men
simply have to go out. It's extremely stupid,
but it's their nature and can't be dodged,
believe me."

"But Mouse, I'm scared. Fafhrd's tale
frightened me. So did yours—I'll hear that
big-headed, black, ratty familiar a-scratch
at the shutters when you're gone, I know I
will!"

It seemed to Fafhrd she was not afraid at all, only taking pleasure in frightening herself and in demonstrating her power over her beloved.

"Darlingest," the Mouser said with a small hiccup, "there is all the Inner Sea, all the Land of the Eight Cities, and to boot all the Trollstep Mountains in their skyscraping grandeur between you and Fafhrd's frigid specters or—pardon me, my comrade, but it could be—hallucinations admixed with coincidences. As for familiars, pish! They've never in the world been anything but the loathy, all-too-natural pets of stinking old women and womanish old men."

"The Eel's but a step, Lady Ivrian," Fafhrd said, "and you'll have beside you my dear Vlana, who slew my chiefest enemy with a single cast of that dagger she now wears."

With a glare at Fafhrd that lasted no longer than a wink, but conveyed "What a way to reassure a frightened girl!" Vlana said merrily, "Let the sillies go, my dear. 'Twill give us chance for a private chat, during which we'll take 'em apart from wine-fumey head to restless foot."

So Ivrian let herself be persuaded and the Mouser and Fafhrd slipped off, quickly shutting the door behind them to keep out the night-smog. Their rather rapid steps down the stairs could clearly be heard from within. There were faint creakings and groanings of the ancient wood outside the wall, but no sound of another tread breaking or other mishap.

Waiting for the four jugs to be brought up from the cellar, the two newly met comrades ordered a mug each of the same fortified wine, or one near enough, and ensconced themselves at the least noisy end of the long serving counter in the tumultuous tavern. The Mouser deftly kicked a rat that thrust black head and shoulders from his hole.

After each had enthusiastically complimented the other on his girl, Fafhrd said diffidently, "Just between ourselves, do you think there might be anything to your sweet Ivrian's notion that the small dark creature with Slivikin and the other Guild-thief was a wizard's familiar, or at any rate the cunning pet of a sorcerer, trained to act as go-between and report disasters to his master or to Krovas or to both?"

The Mouser laughed lightly. "You're building bug-bears—formless baby ones unlicked by logic—out of nothing, dear barbarian brother, if I may say so. *Imprimis*, we don't really know the beastie was connected with the Guild-thieves at all. May well have been a stray catling or a big bold rat—like this damned one!" He kicked again. "But, *secundus*, granting it to be the creature of a wizard employed by Krovas,

how could it make useful report? I don't
believe in animals that talk—except for par-
rots and such birds, which only . . . par-
rot—or ones having an elaborate sign
language men can share. Or perhaps you
envisage the beastie dipping its paddy paw
in a jug of ink and writing its report in big
on a floor-spread parchment?

"Ho, there, you back of the counter!
Where are my jugs? Rats eaten the boy who
went for them days ago? Or he simply
starved to death while on his cellar quest?
Well, tell him to get a swifter move on and
meanwhile brim us again!

"No, Fafhrd, even granting the beastie to
be directly or indirectly a creature of Krovas, and that it raced back to Thieves'
House after our affray, what could it tell
them there? Only that something had gone
wrong with the burglary at Jengao's. Which
they'd soon suspect in any case from the
delay in the thieves' and bravos' return."

Fafhrd frowned and muttered stub-
bornly, "The furry slinker might, nevertheless, convey our appearances to the Guild
masters, and they might recognize us and
come after us and attack us in our homes.
Or Slivikin and his fat pal, revived from
their bumps, might do likewise."

"My dear friend," the Mouser said con-
solingly, "once more begging your indul-
gence, I fear this potent wine is addling
your wits. If the Guild knew our looks or

where we lodge, they'd have been nastily on our necks days, weeks, nay, months ago. Or conceivably you don't know that their penalty for free-lance or even unassigned thieving within the walls of Lankhmar and for three leagues outside them is nothing less than death, after torture if happily that can be achieved."

"I know all about that and my plight is worse even than yours," Fafhrd retorted, and after pledging the Mouser to secrecy told him the tale of Vlana's vendetta against the Guild and her deadly serious dreams of an all-encompassing revenge.

During his story the four jugs came up from the cellar, but the Mouser only ordered that their earthenware mugs be refilled.

Fafhrd finished, "And so, in consequence of a promise given by an infatuated and unschooled boy in a southern angle of the Cold Waste, I find myself now as a sober—well, at other times—man being constantly asked to make war on a power as great as that of Karstak Ovartamortes, for as you may know, the Guild has locals in all other cities and major towns of this land, not to mention agreements including powers of extradition with robber and bandit organizations in other countries. I love Vlana dearly, make no mistake about that, and she is an experienced thief herself, without whose guidance I'd hardly have survived my first week in Lankhmar, but on this one topic she has a kink in her brains, a hard knot neither logic nor persuasion can even begin to loosen. And I, well, in the month I've been here I've learned that the only way to survive in civilization is to abide by its unwritten rules—far more important than its laws chiseled in stone—and break them only at peril, in deepest secrecy, and taking all precautions. As I did tonight—not my first hijacking, by the by."

"Certes 'twould be insanity to assault the Guild direct, your wisdom's perfect there," the Mouser commented. "If you cannot break your most handsome girl of this mad notion, or coax her from it—I can see she's a fearless, self-willed one—then you must stoutly refuse e'en her least request in that direction."

"Certes I must," Fafhrd agreed, adding somewhat accusingly, "though I gather you told her you'd have willingly slit the throats of the two we struck senseless."

"Courtesy merely, man! Would you have had me behave ungraciously to your girl? 'Tis measure of the value I was already setting then on your goodwill. But only a woman's man may cross her. As you must, in this instance."

"Certes I must," Fafhrd repeated with great emphasis and conviction. "I'd be an idiot taking on the Guild. Of course if they should catch me they'd kill me in any case for free-lancing and highjacking. But wantonly to assault the Guild direct, kill one Guild-thief needlessly, only behave as if I might—lunacy entire!"

"You'd not only be a drunken, drooling idiot, you'd questionless be stinking in three nights at most from that emperor of diseases, Death. Malicious attacks on her person, blows directed at the organization, the Guild requites tenfold what she does other rule-breakings. All planned robberies and other thefts would be called off and the entire power of the Guild and its allies mobilized against you alone. I'd count your chances better to take on single-handed the host of the King of Kings rather than the Thieves' Guild's subtle minions. In view of your size, might, and wit you're a squad perhaps, or even a company, but hardly an army. So, no least givings-in to Vlana in this one matter."

"Agreed!" Fafhrd said loudly, shaking the Mouser's iron-thewed hand in a near crusher grip.

"And now we should be getting back to the girls," the Mouser said.

"After one more drink while we settle the score. Ho, boy!"

"Suits." The Mouser dug into his pouch to pay, but Fafhrd protested vehemently. In the end they tossed coin for it, and Fafhrd won and with great satisfaction clinked out his silver smerduks on the stained and dented counter, also marked with an infinitude of mug circles, as if it had been once the desk of a mad geometer. They pushed themselves to their feet, the Mouser giving the rathole one last light kick for luck.

At this, Fafhrd's thoughts looped back and he said, "Grant the beastie can't pawwrite, or talk by mouth or paw, it still could have followed us at distance, marked down your dwelling, and then returned to Thieves' House to lead its masters down on us like a hound!"

"Now you're speaking shrewd sense again," the Mouser said. "Ho, boy, a bucket of small beer to go! On the instant!" Noting Fafhrd's blank look, he explained, "I'll spill it outside the Eel to kill our scent and all the way down the passageway. Yes, and splash it high on the walls too."

Fafhrd nodded wisely. "I thought I'd drunk my way past the addled point."

Vlana and Ivrian, deep in excited talk, both started at the pounding rush of footsteps up the stairs. Racing behemoths could hardly have made more noise. The creaking and groaning were prodigious and there were the crashes of two treads breaking, yet the pounding footsteps never faltered. The door flew open and their two men rushed in through a great mushroom top of nightsmog which was neatly sliced off its black stem by the slam of the door.

"I told you we'd be back in a wink," the

Mouser cried gayly to Ivrian, while Fafhrd strode forward, unmindful of the creaking floor, crying, "Dearest heart, I've missed you sorely," and caught up Vlana despite her voiced protests and pushings-off and kissed and hugged her soundly before setting her back on the couch again.

Oddly, it was Ivrian who appeared to be angry at Fafhrd then, rather than Vlana, who was smiling fondly if somewhat dazedly.

"Fafhrd, sir," she said boldly, her little fists set on her narrow hips, her tapered chin held high, her dark eyes blazing, "my beloved Vlana has been telling me about the unspeakably atrocious things the Thieves' Guild did to her and to her dearest friends. Pardon my frank speaking to one I've only met, but I think it quite unmanly of you to refuse her the just revenge she desires and fully deserves. And that goes for you too, Mouse, who boasted to Vlana of what you would have done had you but known, who in like case did not scruple to slay my very own father—or reputed father—for his cruelties!"

It was clear to Fafhrd that while he and the Gray Mouser had idly boozed in the Eel, Vlana had been giving Ivrian a doubtless empurpled account of her grievances against the Guild and playing mercilessly on the naïve girl's bookish, romantic sympathies and high concept of knightly honor.

It was also clear to him that Ivrian was more than a little drunk. A three-quarters empty flask of violet wine of far Kiraay sat on the low table next to them.

Yet he could think of nothing to do but spread his big hands helplessly and bow his head, more than the low ceiling made necessary, under Ivrian's glare, now reinforced by that of Vlana. After all, they *were* in the right. He *had* promised.

So it was the Mouser who first tried to rebut.

"Come now, pet," he cried lightly as he danced about the room, silk-stuffing more cracks against the thickening night-smog and stirring up and feeding the fire in the stove, "and you too, beauteous Lady Vlana. For the past month Fafhrd has been hitting the Guild-thieves where it hurts them most—in their purses a-dangle between their legs. His highjackings of the loot of their robberies have been like so many fierce kicks in their groins. Hurts worse, believe me, than robbing them of life with a swift, near painless sword slash or thrust. And tonight I helped him in his worthy purpose—and will eagerly do so again. Come, drink we up all." Under his handling, one of the new jugs came uncorked with a pop and he darted about brimming silver cups and mugs.

"A merchant's revenge!" Ivrian retorted with scorn, not one whit appeased, but rather angered anew. "Ye both are at heart true and gentle knights, I know, despite all current backsliding. At the least you must bring Vlana the head of Krovas!"

"What would she *do* with it? What *good* would it be except to spot the carpets?" the Mouser plaintively inquired, while Fafhrd, gathering his wits at last and going down on one knee, said slowly, "Most respected Lady Ivrian, it is true I solemnly promised my beloved Vlana I would help her in her revenge, but that was while I was still in barbarous Cold Corner, where blood-feud is a commonplace, sanctioned by custom and accepted by all the clans and tribes and brotherhoods of the savage Northerners of the Cold Waste. In my naïveté I thought of Vlana's revenge as being of that sort. But here in civilization's midst, I discover all's different and rules and customs turned upside-down. Yet—Lankhmar or Cold Corner—one must seem to observe rule and custom to survive. Here cash is all-powerful, the idol placed highest, whether one sweat, thieve, grind others down, or scheme for it. Here feud and revenge are outside all rules and punished worse than violent lunacy. Think, Lady Ivrian, if Mouse and I should bring Vlana the head of Krovas, she and I would have to flee Lankhmar on the instant, every man's hand against us; while you infallibly would lose this fairyland Mouse has created for love of you and be forced to do likewise, be with him a beggar on the run for the rest of your natural lives."

It was beautifully reasoned and put ... and no good whatsoever. While Fafhrd spoke, Ivrian snatched up her new-filled cup and drained it. Now she stood straight as a soldier, her pale face flushed, and said scathingly to Fafhrd kneeling before her, "*You count the cost!* You speak to me of *things*"—she waved at the many-hued splendor around her—"of mere property, however costly, when *honor* is at stake. You gave Vlana *your word.* Oh, is knighthood wholly dead? And that applies to you, too, Mouse, who swore you'd slit the miserable throats of two noisome Guild-thieves."

"I didn't swear *to,*" the Mouser objected feebly, downing a big drink. "I merely said *I would have,*" while Fafhrd could only shrug again and writhe inside and gulp a little easement from his silver mug. For Ivrian was speaking in the same guilt-showering tones and using the same unfair yet heart-cleaving womanly arguments as Mor his mother might have, or Mara, his deserted Snow Clan sweetheart and avowed wife, big-bellied by now with his child.

In a master stroke, Vlana tried gently to draw Ivrian down to her golden seat again. "Softly, dearest," she pleaded. "You have spoken nobly for me and my cause, and believe me, I am most grateful. Your words

41

revived in me great, fine feelings dead these many years. But of us here, only you are truly an aristocrat attuned to the highest proprieties. We other three are naught but thieves. Is it any wonder some of us put safety above honor and word-keeping, and most prudently avoid risking our lives? Yes, we are three thieves and I am out-voted. So please speak no more of honor and rash, dauntless bravery, but sit you down and—"

"You mean they're both *afraid* to challenge the Thieves' Guild, don't you?" Ivrian said, eyes wide and face twisted by loathing. "I always thought my Mouse was a nobleman first and a thief second. Thieving's nothing. My father lived by cruel thievery done on rich wayfarers and neighbors less powerful than he, yet he was an aristocrat. Oh, you're *cowards*, both of you! *Poltroons!*" she finished, turning her eyes flashing with cold scorn first on the Mouser, then on Fafhrd.

The latter could stand it no longer. He sprang to his feet, face flushed, fists clenched at his sides, quite unmindful of his down-clattered mug and the ominous creak his sudden action drew from the sagging floor.

"*I am not a coward!*" he cried. "I'll dare Thieves' House and fetch you Krovas' head and toss it with blood a-drip at Vlana's feet. I swear that, witness me, Kos the god of

Dooms, by the brown bones of Nalgron my father and by his sword Graywand here at my side!"

He slapped his left hip, found nothing there but his tunic, and had to content himself with pointing tremble-armed at his belt and scabbarded sword where they lay atop his neatly folded robe—and then picking up, refilling splashily, and draining his mug.

The Gray Mouser began to laugh in high, delighted, tuneful peals. All stared at him. He came dancing up beside Fafhrd, and still smiling widely, asked *"Why not?* Who speaks of fearing the Guild-thieves? Who becomes upset at the prospect of this ridiculously easy exploit, when all of us know that all of them, even Krovas and his ruling clique, are but pygmies in mind and skill compared to me or Fafhrd here? A wondrously simple, foolproof scheme has just occurred to me for penetrating Thieves' House, every closet and cranny. Stout Fafhrd and I will put it into effect at once. Are you with me, Northerner?"

"Of course I am," Fafhrd responded gruffly, at the same time frantically wondering what madness had gripped the little fellow.

"Give me a few heartbeats to gather needed props, and we're off!" the Mouser cried. He snatched from a shelf and unfolded a stout sack, then raced about, thrusting into it coiled ropes, bandage rolls, rags, jars of ointment and unction and unguent, and other oddments.

"But you can't go *tonight*," Ivrian protested, suddenly grown pale and uncertain-voiced. "You're both . . . in no condition to."

"You're both *drunk*," Vlana said harshly. "Silly drunk—and that way you'll get naught in Thieves' House but your deaths. Fafhrd, where's that heartless reason you employed to slay or ice-veined see slain a clutch of mighty rivals and win me at Cold Corner and in the chilly, sorcery-webbed depths of Trollstep Canyon? Revive it! And infuse some into your skipping gray friend."

"Oh, no," Fafhrd told her as he buckled on his sword. "You wanted the head of Krovas heaved at your feet in a great splatter of blood, and that's what you're going to get, like it or not!"

"Softly, Fafhrd," the Mouser interjected, coming to a sudden stop and drawing tight the sack's mouth by its strings. "And softly you too, Lady Vlana, and my dear princess. Tonight I intend but a scouting expedition. No risks run, only the information gained needful for planning our murderous strike tomorrow or the day after. So no head-choppings whatsoever tonight, Fafhrd, you hear me? Whatever may hap, hist's the word. And don your hooded robe."

Fafhrd shrugged, nodded, and obeyed.

Ivrian seemed somewhat relieved. Vlana

too, though she said, "Just the same you're both drunk."

"All to the good!" the Mouser assured her with a mad smile. "Drink may slow a man's sword-arm and soften his blows a bit, but it sets his wits ablaze and fires his imagination, and those are the qualities we'll need tonight. Besides," he hurried on, cutting off some doubt Ivrian was about to voice, "drunken men are supremely cautious! Have you ever seen a staggering sot pull himself together at sight of the guard and walk circumspectly and softly past?"

"Yes," Vlana said, "and fall flat on his face just as he comes abreast 'em."

"Pish!" the Mouser retorted and, throwing back his head, grandly walked toward her along an imaginary straight line. Instantly he tripped over his own foot, plunged forward, suddenly without touching floor did an incredible forward flip, heels over head, and landed erect and quite softly—toes, ankles, and knees bending just at the right moment to soak up impact—directly in front of the girls. The floor barely complained.

"You see?" he said, straightening up and unexpectedly reeling backward. He tripped over the pillow on which lay his cloak and sword, but by a wrenching twist and a lurch stayed upright and began rapidly to accouter himself.

Under cover of this action Fafhrd made

quietly yet swiftly to fill once more his and
the Mouser's mugs, but Vlana noted it and
gave him such a glare that he set down
mugs and uncorked jug so swiftly his robe
swirled, then stepped back from the drinks
table with a shrug of resignation and toward Vlana a grimacing nod.

The Mouser shouldered his sack and
drew open the door. With a casual wave at
the girls, but no word spoken, Fafhrd
stepped out on the tiny porch. The night-
smog had grown so thick he was almost lost
to view. The Mouser waved four fingers at
Ivrian, softly called, "Bye-bye, Misling,"
then followed Fafhrd.

"Good fortune go with you," Vlana called
heartily.

"Oh, be careful, Mouse," Ivrian gasped.

The Mouser, his figure slight against the
loom of Fafhrd's, silently drew shut the
door.

Their arms automatically gone around
each other, the girls waited for the inevita-
ble creaking and groaning of the stairs. It
delayed and delayed. The night-smog that
had entered the room dissipated and still
the silence was unbroken.

"What can they be doing out there?"
Ivrian whispered. "Plotting their course?"

Vlana, scowling, impatiently shook her
head, then disentangled herself, tiptoed to
the door, opened it, descended softly a few

steps, which creaked most dolefully, then returned, shutting the door behind her.

"They're gone," she said in wonder, her eyes wide, her hands spread a little to either side, palms up.

"I'm frightened!" Ivrian breathed and sped across the room to embrace the taller girl.

Vlana hugged her tight, then disengaged an arm to shoot the door's three heavy bolts.

In Bones Alley the Mouser returned to his pouch the knotted line by which they'd descended from the lamp hook. He suggested, "How about stopping at the Silver Eel?"

"You mean and just *tell* the girls we've been to Thieves' House?" Fafhrd asked, not too indignantly.

"Oh, no," the Mouser protested. "But you missed your stirrup cup upstairs and so did I."

At the word "stirrup" he looked down at his ratskin boots and then crouching began a little gallop in one place, his boot-soles clopping softly on the cobbles. He flapped imaginary reins—"Giddap!"—and quickened his gallop, but leaning sharply back pulled to a stop—"Whoa!"—when with a crafty smile Fafhrd drew from his robe two full jugs.

"Palmed 'em, as 'twere, when I set down the mugs. Vlana sees a lot, but not all."

"You're a prudent, far-sighted fellow, in

addition to having some skill at sword taps," the Mouser said admiringly. "I'm proud to call you comrade."

Each uncorked and drank a hearty slug. Then the Mouser led them west, they veering and stumbling only a little. Not so far as Cheap Street, however, but turning north into an even narrower and more noisome alley.

"Plague Court," the Mouser said. Fafhrd nodded.

After several preliminary peepings and peerings, they staggered swiftly across wide, empty Crafts Street and into Plague Court again. For a wonder it was growing a little lighter. Looking upward, they saw stars. Yet there was no wind blowing from the north. The air was deathly still.

In their drunken preoccupation with the project at hand and mere locomotion, they did not look behind them. There the night-smog was thicker than ever. A high-circling nighthawk would have seen the stuff converging from all sections of Lankhmar, north, east, south, west—from the Inner Sea, from the Great Salt Marsh, from the many-ditched grainlands, from the River Hlal—in swift-moving black rivers and rivulets, heaping, eddying, swirling, dark and reeking essence of Lankhmar from its branding irons, braziers, bonfires, bonefires, kitchen fires and warmth fires, kilns, forges, breweries, distilleries, junk and gar-

bage fires innumerable, sweating alche-
mists' and sorcerers' dens, crematoriums,
charcoal burners' turfed mounds, all those
and many more ... converging purpose-
fully on Dim Lane and particularly on the
Silver Eel and perhaps especially on the
rickety house behind it, untenanted except
for attic. The closer to that center it got, the
more substantial the smog became, eddy-
strands and swirl-tatters tearing off and
clinging to rough stone corners and
scraggly-surfaced brick like black cobwebs.

But the Mouser and Fafhrd merely ex-
claimed in mild, muted amazement at the
stars, muggily mused as to how much the
improved visibility would increase the risk
of their quest, and cautiously crossing the
Street of the Thinkers, called Atheist Ave-
nue by moralists, continued to Plague Court
until it forked.

The Mouser chose the left branch, which
trended northwest.

"Death Alley."

Fafhrd nodded.

After a curve and recurve, Cheap Street
swung into sight about thirty paces ahead.
The Mouser stopped at once and lightly
threw his arm against Fafhrd's chest.

Clearly in view across Cheap Street was
a wide, low, open doorway, framed by
grimy stone blocks. There led up to it two
steps hollowed by the treadings of centuries. Orange-yellow light spilled out from

bracketed torches inside. They couldn't see very far in because of Death Alley's angle. Yet as far as they *could* see, there was no porter or guard in sight, nor anyone at all, not even a watchdog on a chain. The effect was ominous.

"Now how do we get into the damn place?" Fafhrd demanded in a hoarse whisper. "Scout Murder Alley for a back window that can be forced? You've pries in that sack, I trow. Or try the roof? You're a roof man, I know already. Teach me the art. I know trees and mountains, snow, ice, and bare rock. See this wall here?" He backed off from it, preparing to go up it in a rush.

"Steady on, Fafhrd," the Mouser said, keeping his hand against the big young man's chest. "We'll hold the roof in reserve. Likewise all walls. And I'll take it on trust you're a master climber. As to how we get in, we walk straight through that doorway." He frowned. "Tap and hobble, rather. Come on, while I prepare us."

As he drew the skeptically grimacing Fafhrd back down Death Alley until all Cheap Street was again cut off from view, he explained, "We'll pretend to be beggars, members of *their* guild, which is but a branch of the Thieves' Guild and houses with it, or at any rate reports in to the Beggarmasters at Thieves' House. We'll be new members, who've gone out by day, so it'll not be expected that the Night Beggarmaster and any night watchmen know our looks."

"But we don't look like beggars," Fafhrd protested. "Beggars have awful sores and limbs all atwist or lacking altogether."

"That's just what I'm going to take care of now," the Mouser chuckled, drawing Scalpel. Ignoring Fafhrd's backward step and wary glance, the Mouser gazed puzzledly at the long tapering strip of steel he'd bared, then with a happy nod unclipped from his belt Scalpel's scabbard furbished with ratskin, sheathed the sword and swiftly wrapped it up, hilt and all, in a spiral, with the wide ribbon of a bandage roll dug from his sack.

"There!" he said, knotting the bandage ends. "Now I've a tapping cane."

"What's that?" Fafhrd demanded. "And why?"

"Because I'll be blind, that's why." He took a few shuffling steps, tapping the cobbles ahead with wrapped sword—gripping it by the quillons, or crossguard, so that the grip and pommel were up his sleeve—and groping ahead with his other hand. "That look all right to you?" he asked Fafhrd as he turned back. "Feels perfect to me. Bat-blind, eh? Oh, don't fret, Fafhrd—the rag's but gauze. I can see through it fairly well. Besides, I don't have to convince anyone inside Thieves' House I'm actually blind. Most Guild-beggars fake it, as you must know.

Now what to do with you? Can't have you blind also—too obvious, might wake suspicion." He uncorked his jug and sucked inspiration. Fafhrd copied this action, on principle.

The Mouser smacked his lips and said, "I've got it! Fafhrd, stand on your right leg and double up your left behind you at the knee. Hold! Don't fall on me! Avaunt! But steady yourself by my shoulder. That's right. Now get that left foot higher. We'll disguise your sword like mine, for a crutch cane—it's thicker and'll look just right. You can also steady yourself with your other hand on my shoulder as you hop—the halt leading the blind, always good for a tear, always good theater! But higher with that left foot! No, it just doesn't come off—I'll have to rope it. But first unclip your scabbard."

Soon the Mouser had Graywand and its scabbard in the same state as Scalpel and was tying Fafhrd's left ankle to his thigh, drawing the rope cruelly tight, though Fafhrd's wine-anesthetized nerves hardly registered it. Balancing himself with his steel-cored crutch cane as the Mouser worked, he swigged from his jug and pondered deeply. Ever since joining forces with Vlana, he'd been interested in the theater, and the atmosphere of the actors' tenement had fired that interest further, so that he was delighted at the prospect of acting a part in real life. Yet brilliant as the Mouser's plan undoubtedly was, there did seem to be drawbacks to it. He tried to formulate them.

"Mouser," he said, "I don't know as I like having our swords tied up, so we can't draw 'em in emergency."

"We can still use 'em as clubs," the Mouser countered, his breath hissing between his teeth as he drew the last knot hard. "Besides, we'll have our knives. Say, pull your belt around until yours is behind your back, so your robe will hide it sure. I'll do the same with Cat's Claw. Beggars don't carry weapons, at least in view, and we must maintain dramatic consistency in every detail. Stop drinking now; you've had enough. I myself need only a couple swallows more to reach my finest pitch."

"And I don't know as I like going hobbled into that den of cutthroats. I can hop amazingly fast, it's true, but not as fast as I can run. Is it really wise, think you?"

"You can slash yourself loose in an instant," the Mouser hissed with a touch of impatience and anger. "Aren't you willing to make the least sacrifice for art's sake?"

"Oh, very well," Fafhrd said, draining his jug and tossing it aside. "Yes, of course I am."

"Your complexion's too hale," the Mouser said, inspecting him critically. He touched up Fafhrd's features and hands with pale gray greasepaint, then added wrinkles with dark. "And your garb's too tidy." He scooped dirt from between the cobbles and smeared it on Fafhrd's robe, then tried to put a rip in it, but the material resisted. He shrugged and tucked his lightened sack under his belt.

"So's yours," Fafhrd observed, and stooping on his right leg got a good handful of muck himself, ordure in it by its feel and stink. Heaving himself up with a mighty effort, he wiped the stuff off on the Mouser's cloak and gray silken jerkin too.

The small man got the odor and cursed, but, "Dramatic consistency," Fafhrd reminded him. "It's well we stink. Beggars do—that's one reason folk give 'em coins: to get rid of 'em. And no one at Thieves' House will be eager to inspect us close. Now come on, while our fires are still high." And grasping hold of the Mouser's shoulder, he propelled himself rapidly toward Cheap Street, setting his bandaged sword between cobbles well ahead and taking mighty hops.

"Slow down, idiot," the Mouser cried softly, shuffling along with the speed almost of a skater to keep up, while tapping his (sword) cane like mad. "A cripple's supposed to be *feeble*—that's what draws the sympathy."

Fafhrd nodded wisely and slowed somewhat. The ominous empty doorway slid again into view. The Mouser tilted his jug to get the last of his wine, swallowed awhile, then choked sputteringly. Fafhrd snatched and drained the jug, then tossed it over shoulder to shatter noisily.

They hop-shuffled into Cheap Street, halting almost at once for a richly clad man and woman to pass. The richness of the man's garb was somber and he was on the fat and oldish side, though hard-featured. A merchant doubtless, and with money in the Thieves' Guild—protection money, at least— to take this route at this hour.

The richness of the woman's garb was garish though not tawdry and she was beautiful and young, and looked still younger. A competent courtesan, almost certainly.

The man started to veer around the noisome and filthy pair, his face averted, but the girl swung toward the Mouser, concern growing in her eyes with hothouse swiftness. "Oh, you poor boy! Blind. What tragedy," she said. "Give us a gift for him, lover."

"Keep away from those stinkards, Misra, and come along," he retorted, the last of his speech vibrantly muffled, for he was holding his nose.

She made no reply, but thrust white hand into his ermine pouch and swiftly pressed a coin against the Mouser's palm and closed his fingers on it, then took his head between

55

her palms and kissed him sweetly on the lips before letting herself be dragged on.

"Take good care of the little fellow, old man," she called fondly back to Fafhrd while her companion grumbled muffled reproaches at her, of which only "perverted bitch" was intelligible.

The Mouser stared at the coin in his palm, then sneaked a long look after his benefactress. There was a dazed wonder in his voice as he whispered to Fafhrd, "Look. *Gold*. A golden coin and a beautiful woman's sympathy. Think we should give over this rash project and for a profession take up beggary?"

"Buggery even, rather!" Fafhrd answered harsh and low. That "old man" rankled. "Onward we, bravely!"

They upped the two worn steps and went through the doorway, noting the exceptional thickness of the wall. Ahead was a long, straight, high-ceilinged corridor ending in a stairs and with doors spilling light at intervals and wall-set torches adding their flare, but empty all its length.

They had just got through the doorway when cold steel chilled the neck and pricked a shoulder of each of them. From just above, two voices commanded in unison, "Halt!"

Although fired—and fuddled—by fortified wine, they each had wit enough to freeze and then very cautiously look upward.

Two gaunt, scarred, exceptionally ugly faces, each topped by a gaudy scarf binding back hair, looked down at them from a big, deep niche just above the doorway and helping explain its lowness. Two bent, gnarly arms thrust down the swords that still pricked them.

"Gone out with the noon beggar-batch, eh?" one of them observed. "Well, you'd better have a high take to justify your tardy return. The Night Beggarmaster's on a Whore Street furlough. Report above to Krovas. Gods, you stink! Better clean up first, or Krovas will have you bathed in live steam. Begone!"

The Mouser and Fafhrd shuffled and hobbled forward at their most authentic. One niche-guard cried after them, "Relax, boys! You don't have to put it on here."

"Practice makes perfect," the Mouser called back in a quavering voice. Fafhrd's finger-ends dug his shoulder warningly. They moved along somewhat more naturally, so far as Fafhrd's tied-up leg allowed.

"Gods, what an easy life the Guild-beggars have," the other niche-guard observed to his mate. "What slack discipline and low standards of skill! Perfect, my sacred butt! You'd think a child could see through those disguises."

"Doubtless some children do," his mate

retorted. "But their dear mothers and fathers only drop a tear and a coin or give a kick. Grown folk go blind, lost in their toil and dreams, unless they have a profession such as thieving which keeps them mindful of things as they really are."

Resisting the impulse to ponder this sage philosophy, and glad they would not have to undergo a Beggarmaster's shrewd inspection—truly, thought Fafhrd, Kos of the Dooms seemed to be leading him direct to Krovas and perhaps head-chopping *would* be the order of the night—he and the Mouser went watchfully and slowly on. And now they began to hear voices, mostly curt and clipped ones, and other noises.

They passed some doorways they'd liked to have paused at, to study the activities inside, yet the most they dared do was slow down a bit more. Fortunately most of the doorways were wide, permitting a fairly long view.

Very interesting were some of those activities. In one room young boys were being trained to pick pouches and slit purses. They'd approach from behind an instructor, and if he heard scuff of bare foot or felt touch of dipping hand—or, worst, heard *clunk* of dropped leaden mock-coin—that boy would be thwacked. Others seemed to be getting training in group-tactics: the jostle in front, the snatch from behind, the swift passing of lifted items from youthful thief to confederate.

In a second room, from which pushed air heavy with the reeks of metal and oil, older student thieves were doing laboratory work in lock picking. One group was being lectured by a grimy-handed graybeard, who was taking apart a most complex lock piece by weighty piece. Others appeared to be having their skill, speed, and ability to work soundlessly tested—they were probing with slender picks the keyholes in a half dozen doors set side-by-side in an otherwise purposeless partition, while a supervisor holding a sandglass watched them keenly.

In a third, thieves were eating at long tables. The odors were tempting, even to men full of booze. The Guild did well by its members.

In a fourth, the floor was padded in part and instruction was going on in slipping, dodging, ducking, tumbling, tripping, and otherwise foiling pursuit. These students were older too. A voice like a sergeant-major's rasped, "Nah, nah, nah! You couldn't give your crippled grandmother the slip. I said duck, not genuflect to holy Aarth. Now this time—"

"Grif's used grease," an instructor called.

"He has, eh? To the front, Grif!" the rasping voice replied as the Mouser and Fafhrd moved somewhat regretfully out of sight, for they realized much was to be learned

here: tricks that might stand them in good
stead even tonight. "Listen, all of you!" the
rasping voice continued, so far-carrying it
followed them a surprisingly long way.
"Grease may be very well on a night job—
by day its glisten shouts its user's profession to all Nehwon! But in any case it makes
a thief overconfident. He comes to depend
on it and then in a pinch he finds he's forgot
to apply it. Also its aroma can betray him.
Here we work always dry-skinned—save for
natural sweat!—as all of you were told first
night. Bend over, Grif. Grasp your ankles.
Straighten your knees."

More thwacks, followed by yelps of pain,
distant now, since the Mouser and Fafhrd
were halfway up the end-stairs, Fafhrd vault-
ing somewhat laboriously as he grasped
curving banister and swaddled sword.

The second floor duplicated the first, but
was as luxurious as the other had been
bare. Down the long corridor lamps and fil-
agreed incense pots pendant from the ceiling alternated, diffusing a mild light and
spicy smell. The walls were richly draped,
the floor thick-carpeted. Yet this corridor
was empty too and, moreover, *completely*
silent. After a glance at each other, they
started off boldly.

The first door, wide open, showed an untenanted room full of racks of garments,
rich and plain, spotless and filthy, also wig

stands, shelves of beards and such, and several wall mirrors faced by small tables crowded with cosmetics and with stools before them. A disguising room, clearly.

After a look and listen either way, the Mouser darted in and out to snatch up a large green flask from the nearest table. He unstoppered and sniffed it. A rotten-sweet gardenia-reek contended with the nose-sting of spirits of wine. The Mouser sloshed his and Fafhrd's fronts with this dubious perfume.

"Antidote to ordure," he explained with the pomp of a physician, stoppering the flask. "Don't want to be parboiled by Krovas. No, no, no."

Two figures appeared at the far end of the corridor and came toward them. The Mouser hid the flask under his cloak, holding it between elbow and side, and he and Fafhrd continued onward—to turn back would look suspicious, both drunkenly judged.

The next three doorways they passed were shut by heavy doors. As they neared the fifth, the two approaching figures, coming on arm-in-arm, yet taking long strides, moving more swiftly than the hobble-shuffle, became distinct. Their clothing was that of noblemen, but their faces those of thieves. They were frowning with indignation and suspicion too at the Mouser and Fafhrd.

Just then—from somewhere between the two man-pairs, it sounded—a voice began to speak words in a strange tongue, using the rapid monotone priests employ in a routine service, or some sorcerers in their incantations.

The two richly clad thieves slowed at the seventh doorway and looked in. Their progress ceased altogether. Their necks strained, their eyes widened. They visibly paled. Then of a sudden they hastened onward, almost running, and bypassed Fafhrd and the Mouser as if they were furniture. The incantatory voice drummed on without missing a beat.

The fifth doorway was shut, but the sixth was open. The Mouser peeked in with one eye, his nose brushing the jamb. Then he stepped forward and gazed inside with entranced expression, pushing the black rag up onto his forehead for better vision. Fafhrd joined him.

It was a large room, empty so far as could be told of human and animal life, but filled with most interesting things. From knee-height up, the entire far wall was a map of the city of Lankhmar and its immediate surrounds. Every building and street seemed depicted, down to the meanest hovel and narrowest court. There were signs of recent erasure and redrawing at many spots, and here and there little colored hieroglyphs of mysterious import.

The floor was marble, the ceiling blue as lapis lazuli. The side walls were thickly hung, by ring and padlock. One was covered with all manner of thieves' tools, from a huge thick pry-bar that looked as if it could unseat the universe, or at least the door of the overlord's treasure-vault, to a rod so slim it might be an elf-queen's wand and seemingly designed to telescope out and fish from distance for precious gauds on milady's spindle-legged, ivory-topped vanity table; the other wall had on it all sorts of quaint, gold-gleaming and jewel-flashing objects, evidently mementos chosen for their oddity from the spoils of memorable burglaries, from a female mask of thin gold, breathlessly beautiful in its features and contours, but thickly set with rubies simulating the spots of the pox in its fever-stage, to a knife whose blade was wedge-shaped diamonds set side by side and this diamond cutting-edge looking razor-sharp.

All about were tables set chiefly with models of dwelling houses and other buildings, accurate to the last minutia, it looked, of ventilation hole under roof gutter and ground-level drain hole, of creviced wall and smooth. Many were cut away in partial or entire section to show the layout of rooms, closets, strongrooms, doorways, corridors, secret passages, smoke-ways, and air-ways in equal detail.

Fritz Leiber

In the center of the room was a bare round-table of ebony and ivory squares. About it were set seven straight-backed but well-padded chairs, the one facing the map and away from the Mouser and Fafhrd being higher backed and wider armed than the others—a chief's chair, likely that of Krovas.

The Mouser tiptoed forward, irresistibly drawn, but Fafhrd's left hand clamped down on his shoulder like the iron mitten of a Mingol cataphract and drew him irresistibly back.

Scowling his disapproval, the Northerner brushed down the black rag over the Mouser's eyes again, and with his crutch-hand thumbed ahead; then set off in that direction in most carefully calculated, silent hops. With a shrug of disappointment the Mouser followed.

As soon as they had turned away from the doorway, but before they were out of sight, a neatly black-bearded, crop-haired head came like a serpent's around the side of the highest-backed chair and gazed after them from deep-sunken yet glinting eyes. Next a snake-supple, long hand followed the head out, crossed thin lips with ophidian forefinger for silence, and then finger-beckoned the two pairs of dark-tunicked men who were standing to either side of the doorway, their backs to the corridor wall, each gripping a curvy knife in

64

one hand and a dark leather, lead-weighted bludgeon in the other.

When Fafhrd was halfway to the seventh doorway, from which the monotonous yet sinister recitation continued to well, there shot out through it a slender, whey-faced youth, his narrow hands clapped over his mouth, under terror-wide eyes, as if to shut in screams or vomit, and with a broom clamped in an armpit, so that he seemed a bit like a young warlock about to take to the air. He dashed past Fafhrd and the Mouser and away, his racing footsteps sounding rapid-dull on the carpeting and hollow-sharp on the stairs before dying away.

Fafhrd gazed back at the Mouser with a grimace and shrug, then squatting one-legged until the knee of his bound-up leg touched the floor, advanced half his face past the doorjamb. After a bit, without otherwise changing position, he beckoned the Mouser to approach. The latter slowly thrust half his face past the jamb, just above Fafhrd's.

What they saw was a room somewhat smaller than that of the great map and lit by central lamps that burned blue-white instead of customary yellow. The floor was marble, darkly colorful and complexly whorled. The dark walls were hung with astrological and anthropomantic charts and instruments of magic and shelved with cryptically labeled porcelain jars and also with vitreous flasks and glass pipes of the oddest shapes, some filled with colored fluids, but many gleamingly empty. At the foot of the walls, where the shadows were thickest, broken and discarded stuff was irregularly heaped, as if swept out of the way and forgot, and here and there opened a large rathole.

In the center of the room and brightly illuminated by contrast was a long table with thick top and many stout legs. The Mouser thought fleetingly of a centipede and then of the bar at the Eel, for the tabletop was densely stained and scarred by many a spilled elixir and many a deep black burn by fire or acid or both.

In the midst of the table an alembic was working. The lamp's flame—deep blue, this one—kept a-boil in the large crystal cucurbit a dark, viscid fluid with here and there diamond glints. From out of the thick, seething stuff, strands of a darker vapor streamed upward to crowd through the cucurbit's narrow mouth and stain—oddly, with bright scarlet—the transparent head and then, dead black now, flow down the narrow pipe from the head into a spherical crystal receiver, larger even than the cucurbit, and there curl and weave about like so many coils of living black cord—an endless, skinny, ebon serpent.

Behind the left end of the table stood a

tall, yet hunchbacked man in black robe and hood, which shadowed more than hid a face of which the most prominent features were a long, thick, pointed nose with out-jutting, almost chinless mouth just below. His complexion was sallow-gray like clay and a short-haired, bristly, gray beard grew high on his wide cheeks. From under a receding forehead and bushy gray brows, wide-set eyes looked intently down at an age-browned scroll, which his disgustingly small clubhands, knuckles big, short backs gray-bristled, ceaselessly unrolled and rolled up again. The only move his eyes ever made, besides the short side-to-side one as he read the lines he was rapidly intoning, was an occasional farther sidewise glance at the alembic.

On the other end of the table, beady eyes darting from the sorcerer to the alembic and back again, crouched a small black beast, the first glimpse of which made Fafhrd dig fingers painfully into the Mouser's shoulder and the latter almost gasp, not from the pain. It was most like a rat, yet it had a higher forehead and closer-set eyes than either had ever seen in a rat, while its forepaws, which it constantly rubbed together in what seemed restless glee, looked like tiny copies of the sorcerer's clubhands.

Simultaneously yet independently, Fafhrd and the Mouser each became certain it was the beast which had gutter-escorted

Slivikin and his mate, then fled, and each recalled what Ivrian had said about a witch's familiar and Vlana about the likelihood of Krovas employing a warlock.

What with the ugliness of the clubhanded man and beast and between them the ropy black vapor coiling and twisting in the great receiver and head, like a black umbilical cord, it was a most horrid sight. And the similarities, save for size, between the two creatures were even more disquieting in their implications.

The tempo of the incantation quickened, the blue-white flames brightened and hissed audibly, the fluid in the cucurbit grew thick as lava, great bubbles formed and loudly broke, the black rope in the receiver writhed like a nest of snakes; there was an increasing sense of invisible presences, the supernatural tension grew almost unendurable, and Fafhrd and the Mouser were hard put to keep silent the openmouthed gasps by which they now breathed, and each feared his heartbeat could be heard cubits away.

Abruptly the incantation peaked and broke off, like a drum struck very hard, then instantly silenced by palm and fingers outspread against the head. With a bright flash and dull explosion, cracks innumerable appeared in the cucurbit; its crystal became white and opaque, yet it did not shatter or drip. The head lifted a span, hung there, fell back. While two black nooses appeared among the coils in the receiver and suddenly narrowed until they were only two big black knots.

The sorcerer grinned, rolling up the end of the parchment with a snap, and shifted his gaze from the receiver to his familiar, while the latter chittered shrilly and bounded up and down in rapture.

"Silence, Slivikin! Comes now your time to race and strain and sweat," the sorcerer cried, speaking pidgin Lankhmarese now, but so rapidly and in so squeakingly high-pitched a voice that Fafhrd and the Mouser could barely follow him. They did, however, both realize they had been completely mistaken as to the identity of Slivikin. In moment of disaster, the fat thief had called to the witchbeast for help rather than to his human comrade.

"Yes, master," Slivikin squealed back no less clearly, in an instant revising the Mouser's opinions about talking animals. He continued in the same fifelike, fawning tones, "Harkening in obedience, Hristomilo."

Now they knew the sorcerer's name too.

Hristomilo ordered in whiplash pipings, "To your appointed work! See to it you summon an ample sufficiency of feasters! I want the bodies stripped to skeletons, so the bruises of the enchanted smog and all evidence of death by suffocation will be vanished utterly. But forget not the loot! On your mission, now—depart!"

Slivikin, who at every command had bobbed his head in manner reminiscent of his bouncing, now squealed, "I'll see it done!" and gray-lightninglike leaped a long leap to the floor and down an inky rathole.

Hristomilo, rubbing together his disgusting clubhands much as Slivikin had his, cried chucklingly, "What Slevyas lost, my magic has rewon!"

Fafhrd and the Mouser drew back out of the doorway, partly with the thought that since neither his incantation and his alembic, nor his familiar now required his unblinking attention, Hristomilo would surely look up and spot them; partly in revulsion from what they had seen and heard; and in poignant if useless pity for Slevyas, whoever he might be, and for the other unknown victims of the ratlike and conceivably rat-related sorcerer's deathspells, poor strangers already dead and due to have their flesh eaten from their bones.

Fafhrd wrested the green bottle from the Mouser and, though almost gagging on the rotten-flowery reek, gulped a large, stinging mouthful. The Mouser couldn't quite bring himself to do the same, but was comforted by the spirits of wine he inhaled during this byplay.

Then he saw, beyond Fafhrd, standing before the doorway to the map room, a richly clad man with gold-hilted knife jewel-scabbarded at his side. His sunken-eyed face was prematurely wrinkled by responsibility, overwork, and authority, and framed by neatly cropped black hair and beard. Smiling, he silently beckoned them.

The Mouser and Fafhrd obeyed, the latter returning the green bottle to the former, who recapped it and thrust it under his left elbow with well-concealed irritation.

Each guessed their summoner was Krovas, the Guild's Grandmaster. Once again Fafhrd marveled, as he hobbledehoyed along, reeling and belching, how Kos or the Fates were guiding him to his target tonight. The Mouser, more alert and more apprehensive too, was reminding himself that they had been directed by the niche-guards to report to Krovas, so that the situation, if not developing quite in accord with his own misty plans, was still not deviating disastrously.

Yet not even his alertness, nor Fafhrd's primeval instincts, gave him forewarning as they followed Krovas into the map room.

Two steps inside, each of them was shoulder-grabbed and bludgeon-menaced by a pair of ruffians further armed with knives tucked in their belts.

They judged it wise to make no resistance, on this one occasion at least bearing out the Mouser's mouthings about the supreme caution of drunken men.

"All secure, Grandmaster," one of the ruffians rapped out.

Krovas swung the highest-backed chair around and sat down, eyeing them coolly yet searchingly.

"What brings two stinking, drunken beggar-Guildsmen into the top-restricted precincts of the masters?" he asked quietly.

The Mouser felt the sweat of relief bead his forehead. The disguises he had brilliantly conceived were still working, taking in even the head man, though he had spotted Fafhrd's tipsiness. Resuming his blind-man manner, he quavered, "We were directed by the guard above the Cheap Street door to report to you in person, great Krovas, the Night Beggarmaster being on furlough for reasons of sexual hygiene. Tonight we've made good haul!" And fumbling in his purse, ignoring as far as possible the tightened grip on his shoulders, he brought out the golden coin given him by the sentimental courtesan and displayed it tremble-handed.

"Spare me your inexpert acting," Krovas said sharply. "I'm not one of your marks. And take that rag off your eyes."

The Mouser obeyed and stood to attention again insofar as his pinioning would permit, and smiling the more seeming carefree because of his reawakened uncertainties. Conceivably he wasn't doing quite as brilliantly as he'd thought.

Krovas leaned forward and said placidly yet piercingly, "Granted you were so ordered—and most improperly so; that door-guard will suffer for his stupidity!—why were you spying into a room beyond this one when I spotted you?"

"We saw brave thieves flee from that room," the Mouser answered pat. "Fearing that some danger threatened the Guild, my comrade and I investigated, ready to scotch it."

"But what we saw and heard only perplexed us, great sir," Fafhrd appended quite smoothly.

"I didn't ask you, sot. Speak when you're spoken to," Krovas snapped at him. Then, to the Mouser, "You're an overweening rogue, most presumptuous for your rank."

In a flash the Mouser decided that further insolence, rather than fawning, was what the situation required. "That I am, sir," he said smugly. "For example, I have a master plan whereby you and the Guild might gain more wealth and power in three months than your predecessors have in three millennia."

Krovas' face darkened. "Boy!" he called. Through the curtains of an inner doorway, a youth with dark complexion of a Kleshite and clad only in a black loincloth sprang to kneel before Krovas, who ordered, "Sum-

73

mon first my sorcerer, next the thieves Slevyas and Fissif," whereupon the dark youth
dashed into the corridor.

Then Krovas, his face its normal pale
again, leaned back in his great chair, lightly
rested his sinewy arms on its great padded
ones, and smilingly directed the Mouser,
"Speak your piece. Reveal to us this master
plan."

Forcing his mind *not* to work on the sur-
prising news that Slevyas was not victim
but thief and not sorcery-slain but alive and
available—why did Krovas want him
now?—the Mouser threw back his head
and, shaping his lips in a faint sneer, began,
"You may laugh merrily at me, Grandmaster, but I'll warrant that in less than a
score of heartbeats you'll be straining
sober-faced to hear my least word. Like
lightning, wit can strike anywhere, and
the best of you in Lankhmar have age-
honored blind spots for things obvious to
us of outland birth. My master plan is but
this: let Thieves' Guild under your iron au-
tocracy seize supreme power in Lankhmar
City, then in Lankhmar Land, next over all
Nehwon, after which who knows what
realms undreamt will know your suzer-
ainty!"

The Mouser had spoken true in one respect: Krovas was no longer smiling. He
was leaning forward a little and his face

was darkening again, but whether from interest or anger it was too soon to say.

The Mouser continued, "For centuries the Guild's had more than the force and intelligence needed to make a *coup d'état* a ninefinger certainty; today there's not one hair's chance in a bushy head of failure. It is the proper state of things that thieves rule other men. All Nature cries out for it. No need slay old Karstak Ovartamortes, merely overmaster, control, and so rule through him. You've already fee'd informers in every noble or wealthy house. Your post's better than the King of Kings'. You've a mercenary striking force permanently mobilized, should you have need of it, in the Slayers' Brotherhood. We Guild-beggars are your foragers. O great Krovas, the multitudes know that thievery rules Nehwon, nay, the universe, nay, more, the highest gods' abode! And the multitudes accept this, they balk only at the hypocrisy of the present arrangement, at the pretense that things are otherwise. Oh, give them their decent desire, great Krovas! Make it all open, honest and aboveboard, with thieves ruling in name as well as fact."

The Mouser spoke with passion, for the moment believing all he said, even the contradictions. The four ruffians gaped at him with wonder and not a little awe. They slackened their holds on him and on Fafhrd too.

75

But leaning back in his great chair again and smiling thinly and ominously, Krovas said coolly, "In *our* Guild intoxication is no excuse for folly, rather grounds for the extremest penalty. But I'm well aware your organized beggars operate under a laxer discipline. So I'll deign to explain to you, you wee drunken dreamer, that we thieves know well that, behind the scenes, we already rule Lankhmar, Nehwon, all life in sooth—for what is life but greed in action? But to make this an open thing would not only force us to take on ten thousand sorts of weary work others now do for us, it would also go against another of life's deep laws: illusion. Does the sweetmeats hawker show you his kitchen? Does a whore let average client watch her enamel-over her wrinkles and hoist her sagging breasts in cunning gauzy slings? Does a conjuror turn out for you his hidden pockets? Nature works by subtle, secret means—man's invisible seed, spider bite, the viewless spores of madness and of death, rocks that are born in earth's unknown bowels, the silent stars a-creep across the sky—and we thieves copy her."

"That's good enough poetry, sir," Fafhrd responded with undertone of angry derision, for he had himself been considerably impressed by the Mouser's master plan and was irked that Krovas should do insult to his new friend by disposing of it so lightly.

"Closet kingship may work well enough in easy times. But"—he paused histrionically—"will it serve when Thieves' Guild is faced with an enemy determined to obliterate it forever, a plot to wipe it entirely from the earth?"

"What drunken babble's this?" Krovas demanded, sitting up straight. "*What* plot?"

" 'Tis a most *secret* one," Fafhrd responded, grinning, delighted to pay this haughty man in his own coin and thinking it quite just that the thief-king sweat a little before his head was removed for conveyance to Vlana. "I know naught of it, except that many a master thief is marked down for the knife—and your head doomed to fall!"

Fafhrd merely sneered his face and folded his arms, the still slack grip of his captors readily permitting it, his (sword) crutch hanging against his body from his lightly gripping hand. Then he scowled as there came a sudden shooting pain in his numbed, bound-up leg, which he had forgotten for a space.

Krovas raised a clenched fist and himself half out of his chair, in prelude to some fearsome command—likely that Fafhrd be tortured. The Mouser cut in hurriedly with, "The Secret Seven, they're called, are its leaders. None in the outer circles of the conspiracy know their names, though rumor has it that they're secret Guild-thief renegades representing, one for each, the cities of Ool Hrusp, Kvarch Nar, Ilthmar, Horborixen, Tisilinilit, far Kiraay and Lankhmar's very self. It's thought they're moneyed by the merchants of the East, the priests of Wan, the sorcerers of the Steppes and half the Mingol leadership too, legended Quarmall, Aarth's Assassins in Sarheenmar, and also no lesser man than the King of Kings."

Despite Krovas' contemptuous and then angry remarks, the ruffians holding the Mouser continued to harken to their captive with interest and respect, and they did not retighten their grip on him. His colorful revelations and melodramatic delivery held them, while Krovas' dry, cynical, philosophic observations largely went over their heads.

Hristomilo came gliding into the room then, his feet presumably taking swift, but very short steps; at any rate his black robe hung undisturbed to the marble floor despite his slithering speed.

There was a shock at his entrance. All eyes in the map room followed him, breaths were held, and the Mouser and Fafhrd felt the horny hands that gripped them shake just a little. Even Krovas' all-confident, world-weary expression became tense and guardedly uneasy. Clearly the sorcerer of the Thieves' Guild was more feared than

loved by his chief employer and by the ben-
eficiaries of his skills.

Outwardly oblivious to this reaction to
his appearance, Hristomilo, smiling thin-
lipped, halted close to one side of Krovas'
chair and inclined his hood-shadowed rodent face in the ghost of a bow.

Krovas held palm toward the Mouser for
silence. Then, wetting his lips, he asked
Hristomilo sharply yet nervously, "Do you
know these two?"

Hristomilo nodded decisively. "They just
now peered a befuddled eye each at me,"
he said, "whilst I was about that business
we spoke of. I'd have shooed them off, reported them, save such action might have
broken my spell, put my words out of time
with the alembic's workings. The one's a
Northerner, the other's features have a
southern cast—from Tovilyis or near, most
like. Both younger than their now-looks.
Free-lance bravos, I'd judge 'em, the sort
the Brotherhood hires as extras when they
get at once several big guard and escort
jobs. Clumsily disguised now, of course, as
beggars."

Fafhrd by yawning, the Mouser by pity-
ing headshake tried to convey that all this
was so much poor guesswork.

"That's all I can tell you without reading
their minds," Hristomilo concluded. "Shall
I fetch my lights and mirrors?"

"Not yet." Krovas turned face and shot a

finger at the Mouser. "How do you know these things you rant about?—Secret Seven and all. Straight simplest answer now—no rodomontades."

The Mouser replied most glibly: "There's a new courtesan dwells on Pimp Street— Tyarya her name, tall, beauteous, but hunchbacked, which oddly delights many of her clients. Now Tyarya loves me 'cause my maimed eyes match her twisted spine, or from simple pity of my blindness—*she* believes it!—and youth, or from some odd itch, like her clients' for her, which that combination arouses in her flesh.

"Now one of her patrons, a trader newly come from Klelg Nar—Mourph, he's called—was impressed by my intelligence, strength, boldness, and closemouthed tact, and those same qualities in my comrade too. Mourph sounded us out, finally asking if we hated the Thieves' Guild for its control of the Beggars' Guild. Sensing a chance to aid the Guild, we played up, and a week ago he recruited us into a cell of three in the outermost strands of the conspiracy web of the Seven."

"You presumed to do all of this on your own?" Krovas demanded in freezing tones, sitting up straight and gripping hard the chair arms.

"Oh, no," the Mouser denied guilelessly. "We reported our every act to the Day Beggarmaster and he approved them, told us to spy our best and gather every scrap of fact and rumor we could about the Sevens' conspiracy."

"And he told me not a word about it!" Krovas rapped out. "If true, I'll have Bannat's head for this! But you're lying, aren't you?"

As the Mouser gazed with wounded eyes at Krovas, meanwhile preparing a most virtuous denial, a portly man limped past the doorway with help of a gilded staff. He moved with silence and aplomb.

But Krovas saw him. "Night Beggarmaster!" he called sharply. The limping man stopped, turned, came crippling majestically through the door. Krovas stabbed finger at the Mouser, then Fafhrd. "Do you know these two, Flim?"

The Night Beggarmaster unhurriedly studied each for a space, then shook his head with its turban of cloth of gold. "Never seen either before. What are they? Fink beggars?"

"But Flim wouldn't know us," the Mouser explained desperately, feeling everything collapsing in on him and Fafhrd. "All our contacts were with Bannat alone."

Flim said quietly, "Bannat's been abed with the swamp ague this past ten-day. Meanwhile *I* have been Day Beggarmaster as well as Night."

At that moment Slevyas and Fissif came hurrying in behind Flim. The tall thief bore on his jaw a bluish lump. The fat thief's head was bandaged above his darting eyes. He pointed quickly at Fafhrd and the Mouser and cried, "There are the two that slugged us, took our Jengao loot, and slew our escort."

The Mouser lifted his elbow and the green bottle crashed to shards at his feet on the hard marble. Gardenia-reek sprang swiftly through the air.

But more swiftly still the Mouser, shaking off the careless hold of his startled guards, sprang toward Krovas, clubbing his wrapped-up sword. If he could only overpower the King of Thieves and hold Cat's Claw at his throat, he'd be able to bargain for his and Fafhrd's lives. That is, unless the other thieves wanted their master killed, which wouldn't surprise him at all.

With startling speed Flim thrust out his gilded staff, tripping the Mouser, who went heels over head, midway seeking to change his involuntary somersault into a voluntary one.

Meanwhile Fafhrd lurched heavily against his left-hand captor, at the same time swinging bandaged Graywand strongly upward to strike his right-hand captor under the jaw. Regaining his one-legged balance with a mighty contortion, he hopped for the loot-wall behind him.

Slevyas made for the wall of thieves' tools, and with a muscle-cracking effort wrenched the great pry-bar from its pad-locked ring.

Scrambling to his feet after a poor landing in front of Krovas' chair, the Mouser found it empty and the Thief King in a half-crouch behind it, gold-hilted dagger drawn, deep-sunk eyes coldly battle-wide. Spinning around, he saw Fafhrd's guards on the floor, the one sprawled senseless, the other starting to scramble up, while the great Northerner, his back against the wall of weird jewelry, menaced the whole room with wrapped-up Graywand and with his long knife, jerked from its scabbard behind him.

Likewise drawing Cat's Claw, the Mouser cried in trumpet voice of battle, "Stand aside, all! He's gone mad! I'll hamstring his good leg for you!" And racing through the press and between his own two guards, who still appeared to hold him in some awe, he launched himself with flashing dirk at Fafhrd, praying that the Northerner, drunk now with battle as well as wine and poisonous perfume, would recognize him and guess his stratagem.

Graywand slashed well above his ducking head. His new friend not only guessed, but was playing up—and not just missing by accident, the Mouser hoped. Stooping low by the wall, he cut the lashings on Fafhrd's left leg. Graywand and Fafhrd's long knife continued to spare him. Springing up, he headed for the corridor, crying over-shoulder to Fafhrd, "Come on!"

Hristomilo stood well out of the way, quietly observing. Fissif scuttled toward safety. Krovas stayed behind his chair, shouting, "Stop them! Head them off!"

The three remaining ruffian guards, at last beginning to recover their fighting-wits, gathered to oppose the Mouser. But menacing them with swift feints of his dirk, he slowed them and darted between—and then just in the nick of time knocked aside with a downsweep of wrapped-up Scalpel Flim's gilded staff, thrust once again to trip him.

All this gave Slevyas time to return from the tools-wall and aim at the Mouser a great swinging blow with the massive pry-bar. But even as that blow started, a very long, bandaged sword on a very long arm thrust over the Mouser's shoulder and solidly and heavily poked Slevyas high on the chest, jolting him backward, so that the pry-bar's swing was short and whistled past harmlessly.

Then the Mouser found himself in the corridor and Fafhrd beside him, though for some weird reason still only hopping. The Mouser pointed toward the stairs. Fafhrd nodded, but delayed to reach high, still on one leg only, and rip off the nearest wall a dozen cubits of heavy drapes, which he threw across the corridor to baffle pursuit.

They reached the stairs and started up

the next flight, the Mouser in advance. There were cries behind, some muffled.

"Stop hopping, Fafhrd!" the Mouser ordered querulously. "You've got two legs again."

"Yes, and the other's still dead," Fafhrd complained. "Ahh! Now feeling begins to return to it."

A thrown knife whisked between them and dully clinked as it hit the wall point-first and stone-powder flew. Then they were around the bend.

Two more empty corridors, two more curving flights, and then they saw above them on the last landing a stout ladder mounting to a dark square hole in the roof. A thief with hair bound back by a colorful handkerchief—it appeared to be a door-guards' identification—menaced the Mouser with drawn sword, but when he saw that there were two of them, both charging him determinedly with shining knives and strange staves or clubs, he turned and ran down the last empty corridor.

The Mouser, followed closely by Fafhrd, rapidly mounted the ladder and without pause vaulted up through the hatch into the star-crusted night.

He found himself near the unrailed edge of a slate roof which slanted enough to have made it look most fearsome to a novice roof-walker, but safe as houses to a veteran.

Crouched on the long peak of the roof was another kerchiefed thief holding a dark lantern. He was rapidly covering and uncovering, presumably in some code, the lantern's bull's-eye, whence shot a faint green beam north to where a red point of light winked dimly in reply—as far away as the sea wall, it looked, or perhaps the masthead of a ship beyond, riding in the Inner Sea. Smuggler?

Seeing the Mouser, this one instantly drew sword and, swinging the lantern a little in his other hand, advanced menacingly. The Mouser eyed him warily—the dark lantern with its hot metal, concealed flame, and store of oil would be a tricky weapon.

But then Fafhrd had clambered out and was standing beside the Mouser, on both feet again at last. Their adversary backed slowly away toward the north end of the roof ridge. Fleetingly the Mouser wondered if there was another hatch there.

Turning back at a bumping sound, he saw Fafhrd prudently hoisting the ladder. Just as he got it free, a knife flashed up close past him out of the hatch. While following its flight, the Mouser frowned, involuntarily admiring the skill required to hurl a knife vertically with any accuracy.

It clattered down near them and slid off the roof. The Mouser loped south across the slates and was halfway from the hatch to that end of the roof when the faint chink came of the knife striking the cobbles of Murder Alley.

Fafhrd followed more slowly, in part perhaps from a lesser experience of roofs, in part because he still limped a bit to favor his left leg, and in part because he was carrying the heavy ladder balanced on his right shoulder.

"We won't need that," the Mouser called back.

Without hesitation Fafhrd heaved it joyously over the edge. By the time it crashed in Murder Alley, the Mouser was leaping down two yards and across a gap of one to the next roof, of opposite and lesser pitch. Fafhrd landed beside him.

The Mouser led them at almost a run through a sooty forest of chimneys, chimney pots, ventilators with tails that made them always face the wind, black-legged cisterns, hatch covers, bird houses, and pigeon traps across five roofs, four progressively a little lower, the fifth regaining a yard of the altitude they'd lost—the spaces between the buildings easy to leap, none more than three yards, no ladder-bridge required, and only one roof with a somewhat greater pitch than that of Thieves' House—until they reached the Street of the Thinkers at a point where it was crossed by a

roofed passageway much like the one at
Rokkermas and Slaarg's.

While they crossed it at a crouching lope,
something hissed close past them and clattered ahead. As they leaped down from the
roof of the bridge, three somethings hissed
over their heads to clatter beyond. One re-
bounded from a square chimney almost to
the Mouser's feet. He picked it up, expecting a stone, and was surprised by the
greater weight of a leaden ball big as two
doubled-up fingers.

"They," he said, jerking thumb over-
shoulder, "lost no time in getting slingers
on the roof. When roused, they're good."

Southeast then through another black
chimney-forest to a point on Cheap Street
where upper stories overhung the street so
much on either side that it was easy to leap
the gap. During this roof-traverse, an ad-
vancing front of night-smog, dense enough
to make them cough and wheeze, had engulfed them and for perhaps sixty heartbeats the Mouser had had to slow to a
shuffle and feel his way, Fafhrd's hand on
his shoulder. Just short of Cheap Street
they had come abruptly and completely out
of the smog and seen the stars again, while
the black front had rolled off northward behind him.

"Now what the devil was that?" Fafhrd
had asked and the Mouser had shrugged.

A nighthawk would have seen a vast thick

hoop of black night-smog blowing out in all directions from a center near the Silver Eel, growing ever greater and greater in diameter and circumference.

East of Cheap Street the two comrades soon made their way to the ground, landing back in Plague Court behind the narrow premises of Nattick Nimblefingers the Tailor.

Then at last they looked at each other and their trammeled swords and their filthy faces and clothing made dirtier still by roof-soot, and they laughed and laughed and laughed, Fafhrd roaring still as he bent over to massage his left leg above and below knee. This hooting and wholly unaffected self-mockery continued while they unwrapped their swords—the Mouser as if his were a surprise package—and clipped their scabbards once more to their belts. Their exertions had burned out of them the last mote and atomy of strong wine and even stronger stenchful perfume, but they felt no desire whatever for more drink, only the urge to get home and eat hugely and guzzle hot, bitter gahveh, and tell their lovely girls at length the tale of their mad adventure.

They loped on side by side, at intervals glancing at each other and chuckling, though keeping a normally wary eye behind and before for pursuit or interception, despite their expecting neither.

Free of night-smog and drizzled with starlight, their cramped surroundings seemed much less stinking and oppressive than when they had set out. Even Ordure Boulevard had a freshness to it.

Only once for a brief space did they grow serious.

Fafhrd said, "You were drunken idiot-genius indeed tonight, even if I was a drunken clodhopper. Lashing up my leg! Tying up our swords so we couldn't use 'em save as clubs!"

The Mouser shrugged. "Yet that sword-tying doubtless saved us from committing a number of murders tonight."

Fafhrd retorted, a little hotly, "Killing in a fight isn't murder."

Again the Mouser shrugged. "Killing is murder, no matter what nice names you give. Just as eating is devouring, and drinking guzzling. Gods, I'm dry, famished, and fatigued! Come on, soft cushions, food, and steaming gahveh!"

They hastened up the long, creaking, broken treaded stairs with an easy carefulness and when they were both on the porch, the Mouser shoved at the door to open it with surprise-swiftness.

It did not budge.

"Bolted," he said to Fafhrd shortly. He noted now there was hardly any light at all coming through the cracks around the door, or noticeable through the lattices—at most, a faint orange-red glow. Then with sentimental grin and in a fond voice in which only the ghost of uneasiness lurked, he said, "They've gone to sleep, the unworrying wenches!" He knocked loudly thrice and then cupping his lips shouted softly at the door crack, "Hola, Ivrian! I'm home safe. Hail, Vlana! Your man's done you proud, felling Guild-thieves innumerable with one foot tied behind his back!"

There was no sound whatever from inside—that is, if one discounted a rustling so faint it was impossible to be sure of it.

Fafhrd was wrinkling his nostrils. "I smell smoke."

The Mouser banged on the door again. Still no response.

Fafhrd motioned him out of the way, hunching his big shoulder to crash the portal.

The Mouser shook his head and with a deft tap, slide, and tug removed a brick that a moment before had looked a firm-set part of the wall beside the door. He reached in all his arm. There was the scrape of a bolt being withdrawn, then another, then a third. He swiftly recovered his arm and the door swung fully inward at a touch.

But neither he nor Fafhrd rushed in at once, as both had intended to, for the indefinable scent of danger and the unknown came puffing out along with an increased reek of smoke and a slight sickening sweet scent that though female was no decent female perfume, and a musty-sour animal odor.

They could see the room faintly by the orange glow coming from the small oblong of the open door of the little, well-blacked stove. Yet the oblong did not sit properly upright but was unnaturally a-tilt; clearly the stove had been half overset and now leaned against a side wall of the fireplace, its small door fallen open in that direction.

By itself alone, that unnatural angle conveyed the entire impact of a universe overturned.

The orange glow showed the carpets oddly rucked up with here and there black circles a palm's breadth across, the neatly stacked candles scattered about below their shelves along with some of the jars and enameled boxes, and, above all, two black, low, irregular, longish heaps, the one by the fireplace, the other half on the golden couch, half at its foot.

From each heap there stared at the Mouser and Fafhrd innumerable pairs of tiny, rather widely set, furnace-red eyes.

On the thickly carpeted floor on the other side of the fireplace was a silver cobweb—a fallen silver cage, but no love birds sang from it.

There was a faint scrape of metal as Fafhrd made sure Graywand was loose in his scabbard.

As if that tiny sound had beforehand been

chosen as the signal for attack, each instantly whipped out sword and they advanced side by side into the room, warily at first, testing the floor with each step.

At the screech of the swords being drawn, the tiny furnace-red eyes had winked and shifted restlessly, and now with the two men's approach they swiftly scattered, pattering, pair by red pair, each pair at the forward end of a small, low, slender, hairless-tailed black body, and each making for one of the black circles in the rugs, where they vanished.

Indubitably the black circles were rat-holes newly gnawed up through the floor and rugs, while the red-eyed creatures were black rats.

Fafhrd and the Mouser sprang forward, slashing and chopping at them in a frenzy, cursing and human-snarling besides.

They sundered few. The rats fled with preternatural swiftness, most of them disappearing down holes near the walls and the fireplace.

Also Fafhrd's first frantic chop went through the floor and on his third step with an ominous crack and splintering his leg plunged through the floor to his hip. The Mouser darted past him, unmindful of further crackings.

Fafhrd heaved out his trapped leg, not even noting the splinter-scratches it got and as unmindful as the Mouser of the continuing creakings. The rats were gone. He lunged after his comrade, who had thrust a bunch of kindlers into the stove, to make more light.

The horror was that, although the rats were all gone, the two longish heaps remained, although considerably diminished and, as now shown clearly by the yellow flames leaping from the tilted black door, changed in hue, no longer were the heaps red-beaded black, but a mixture of gleaming black and dark brown, a sickening purple-blue, violet and velvet black and ermine white, and the reds of stockings and blood and bloody flesh and bone.

Although hands and feet had been gnawed bone-naked, and bodies tunneled heart-deep, the two faces had been spared. That was not good, for they were the parts purple-blue from death by strangulation, lips drawn back, eyes bulging, all features contorted in agony. Only the black and very dark brown hair gleamed unchanged—that and the white, white teeth.

As each man stared down at his love, unable to look away despite the waves of horror and grief and rage washing higher and higher in him, each saw a tiny black strand uncurl from the black depression ringing each throat and drift off, dissipating, toward the open door behind them—two strands of night-smog.

With a crescendo of crackings the floor

sagged fully three spans more in the center before arriving at a new temporary stability.

Edges of centrally tortured minds noted details: that Vlana's silver-hilted dagger skewered to the floor a rat, which, likely enough, overeager had approached too closely before the night-smog had done its magic work. That her belt and pouch were gone. That the blue-enameled box inlaid with silver, in which Ivrian had put the Mouser's share of the highjacked jewels, was gone too.

The Mouser and Fafhrd lifted to each other white, drawn faces which were quite mad, yet completely joined in understanding and purpose. No need to tell each other what must have happened here when the two nooses of black vapor had jerked tight in Hristomilo's receiver, or why Slivikin had bounced and squeaked in glee, or the significance of such phrases as "an ample sufficiency of feasters," or "forget not the loot," or "that business we spoke of." No need for Fafhrd to explain why he now stripped off his robe and hood, or why he jerked up Vlana's dagger, snapped the rat off it with a wrist-flick, and thrust it in his belt. No need for the Mouser to tell why he searched out the half dozen jars of oil and after smashing three of them in front of the flaming stove, paused, thought, and stuck the other three in the sack at his waist, adding to them the remaining kindlers and the fire-pot, brimmed with red coals, its top lashed down tight.

Then, still without a word exchanged, the Mouser muffled his hand with a small rug and reaching into the fireplace deliberately tipped the flaming stove forward, so that it fell door-down on oil-soaked rugs. Yellow flames sprang up around him.

They turned and raced for the door. With louder crackings than any before, the floor collapsed. They desperately scrambled their way up a steep hill of sliding carpets and reached door and porch just before all behind them gave way and the flaming rugs and stove and all the firewood and candles and the golden couch and all the little tables and boxes and jars—and the unthinkably mutilated bodies of their first loves—cascaded into the dry, dusty, cobweb-choked room below, and the great flames of a cleansing or at least obliterating cremation began to flare upward.

They plunged down the stairs, which tore away from the wall and collapsed and dully crashed in the dark just as they reached the ground. They had to fight their way over the wreckage to get to Bones Alley.

By then flames were darting their bright lizard-tongues out of the shuttered attic windows and the boarded-up ones in the story just below. By the time they reached Plague Court, running side by side at top speed, the Silver Eel's fire-alarm was clanging cacophonously behind them.

They were still sprinting when they took the Death Alley fork. Then the Mouser grappled Fafhrd and forced him to a halt. The big man struck out, cursing insanely, and only desisted—his white face still a lunatic's—when the Mouser cried, panting, "Only ten heartbeats to arm us!"

He pulled the sack from his belt and, keeping tight hold of its neck, crashed it on the cobbles—hard enough to smash not only the bottles of oil, but also the fire-pot, for the sack was soon flaming a little at its base.

Then he drew gleaming Scalpel and Fafhrd Graywand and they raced on, the Mouser swinging his sack in a great circle beside him to fan its flames. It was a veritable ball of fire burning in his left hand as they dashed across Cheap Street and into Thieves' House, and the Mouser, leaping high, swung it up into the great niche above the doorway and let go of it.

The niche-guards screeched in surprise and pain at the fiery invader of their hidey-hole and had no time to do anything with their swords, or whatever weapons else they had, against the two invaders.

Student thieves poured out of the doors ahead at the screeching and foot-pounding, and then poured back as they saw the fierce point of flames and the two demon-faced oncomers brandishing their long, shining swords.

One skinny little apprentice—he could hardly have been ten years old—lingered too long. Graywand thrust him pitilessly through as his big eyes bulged and his small mouth gaped in horror and plea to Fafhrd for mercy.

Now from ahead of them there came a weird, wailing call, hollow and hair-raising, and doors began to thus shut instead of spewing forth the armed guards they almost prayed would appear to be skewered by their swords. Also, despite the long, bracketed torches looking newly released, the corridor was dark.

The reason for this last became clear as they plunged up the stairs. Strands of night-smog were appearing in the well, materializing from nothing or the air.

The strands grew longer and more numerous and tangible. They touched and clung nastily. In the corridor above they were forming from wall to wall and from ceiling to floor, like a gigantic cobweb, and were becoming so substantial that the Mouser and Fafhrd had to slash them to get through, or so their two maniac minds believed. The black web muffled a little a repetition of the eerie, wailing call, which came from the seventh door ahead and this time ended in a gleeful chittering and cackling insane as the emotions of the two attackers.

Here too doors were thudding shut. In an ephemeral flash of rationality, it occurred to the Mouser that it was not he and Fafhrd the thieves feared, for they had not been seen yet, but rather Hristomilo and his magic, even though working in defense of Thieves' House.

Even the map room, whence counter-attack would most likely erupt, was closed off by a huge oaken, iron-studded door.

They were now twice slashing black, clinging rope-thick spiderweb for every single step they drove themselves forward. Midway between the map and magic rooms, there was forming on the inky web, ghostly at first but swiftly growing more substantial, a black spider big as a wolf.

The Mouser slashed heavy cobweb before it, dropped back two steps, then hurled himself at it in a high leap. Scalpel thrust through it, striking amidst its eight new-formed jet eyes, and it collapsed like a daggered bladder, loosing a vile stink.

Then he and Fafhrd were looking into the magic room, the alchemist's chamber. It was much as they had seen it before, except some things were doubled, or multiplied even further.

On the long table two blue-boiled cucur-bits bubbled and roiled, their heads shoot-ing out a solid, writhing rope more swiftly than moves the black swamp-cobra, which can run down a man—and not into twin receivers, but into the open air of the room (if any of the air in Thieves' House could have been called open then) to weave a barrier between their swords and Hristomilo, who once more stood tall though hunchbacked over his sorcerous, brown parchment, though this time his exultant gaze was chiefly fixed on Fafhrd and the Mouser, with only an occasional downward glance at the text of the spell he drummingly intoned.

At the other end of the table, in the web-free space, there bounced not only Slivikin, but also a huge rat matching him in size in all members except the head.

From the ratholes at the foot of the walls, red eyes glittered and gleamed in pairs.

With a bellow of rage Fafhrd began slashing at the black barrier, but the ropes were replaced from the cucurbit heads as swiftly as he sliced them, while the cut ends, instead of drooping slackly, now began to strain hungrily toward him like constrictive snakes or strangle-vines.

He suddenly shifted Graywand to his left hand, drew his long knife and hurled it at the sorcerer. Flashing toward its mark, it cut through three strands, was deflected and slowed by a fourth and fifth, almost halted by a sixth, and ended hanging futilely in the curled grip of a seventh.

Hristomilo laughed cacklingly and grinned, showing his huge upper incisors, while Slivikin chittered in ecstasy and bounded the higher.

The Mouser hurled Cat's Claw with no better result—worse, indeed, since his action gave two darting smog-strands time to curl hamperingly around his sword-hand and stranglingly around his neck. Black rats came racing out of the big holes at the cluttered base of the walls.

Meanwhile other strands snaked around Fafhrd's ankles, knees and left arm, almost toppling him. But even as he fought for balance, he jerked Vlana's dagger from his belt and raised it over his shoulder, its silver hilt glowing, its blade brown with dried rat's-blood.

The grin left Hristomilo's face as he saw it. The sorcerer screamed strangely and importuningly then and drew back from his parchment and the table, and raised clawed clubhands to ward off doom.

Vlana's dagger sped unimpeded through the black web—its strands even seemed to part for it—and betwixt the sorcerer's warding hands, to bury itself to the hilt in his right eye.

He screamed thinly in dire agony and clawed at his face.

The black web writhed as if in death spasm.

The cucurbits shattered as one, spilling their lava on the scarred table, putting out the blue flames even as the thick wood of the table began to smoke a little at the lava's edge. Lava dropped with *plops* on the dark marble floor.

With a faint, final scream Hristomilo pitched forward, hands still clutched to his eyes above his jutting nose, silver dagger-hilt still protruding between his fingers.

The web grew faint, like wet ink washed with a gush of clear water.

The Mouser raced forward and transfixed Slivikin and the huge rat with one thrust of Scalpel before the beasts knew what was happening. They too died swiftly with thin screams, while all the other rats turned tail and fled back down their holes swift almost as black lightning.

Then the last trace of night-smog or sorcery-smoke vanished and Fafhrd and the Mouser found themselves standing alone with three dead bodies and a profound silence that seemed to fill not only this room but all Thieves' House. Even the cucurbit-lava had ceased to move, was hardening, and the wood of the table no longer smoked.

Their madness was gone and all their rage too—vented to the last red atomy and glutted to more than satiety. They had no more urge to kill Krovas or any other of the thieves than to swat flies. With horrified inner eye Fafhrd saw the pitiful face of the child-thief he'd skewered in his lunatic anger.

Only their grief remained with them, diminished not one whit, but rather growing greater—that and an ever more swiftly growing revulsion from all that was around them: the dead, the disordered magic room, all Thieves' House, all of the city of Lankhmar to its last stinking alleyway and smog-wreathed spire.

With a hiss of disgust the Mouser jerked Scalpel from the rodent cadavers, wiped it on the nearest cloth, and returned it to its scabbard. Fafhrd likewise sketchily cleansed and sheathed Graywand. Then the two men picked up their knife and dirk from where they'd dropped to the floor when the web had dematerialized, though neither so much as glanced at Vlana's dagger where it was buried. But on the sorcerer's table they did notice Vlana's black velvet, silver-worked pouch and belt, the latter half overrun by the hardened black lava, and Ivrian's blue-enameled box inlaid with silver. From these they took the gems of Jengao.

With no more word than they had exchanged back at the Mouser's burned nest behind the Eel, but with a continuing sense of their unity of purpose, their identity of intent, and of their comradeship, they made their way with shoulders bowed and with slow, weary steps which only very gradually quickened out of the magic room and down the thick-carpeted corridor, past the map room's wide door still barred with oak and iron, and past all the other shut, silent doors—clearly the entire Guild was terrified of Hristomilo, his spells, and his rats; down the echoing stairs, their footsteps resounding loudly no matter how softly they sought to tread; under the deserted, black-scorched guard-niche, and so out into Cheap Street, turning left and north because that was the nearest way to the Street of the Gods, and there turning right and east—not a waking soul in the wide street except for one skinny, bent-backed apprentice lad unhappily swabbing the flagstones in front of a wine shop in the dim pink light beginning to seep from the east, although there were many forms asleep, a-snore and a-dream in the gutters and under the dark porticos—yes, turning right and east down the Street of the Gods, for that way was the Marsh Gate, leading to Causey Road across the Great Salt Marsh, and the Marsh Gate was the nearest way out of the great and glamorous city that was now loathsome to them, indeed, not to be endured for one more stabbing, leaden heartbeat than was necessary—a city of beloved, unfaceable ghosts.

THE TOR DOUBLES

Two complete short science fiction novels in one volume!

MORE OF THE FINEST IN
SHORT HORROR STORIES

RED RAGE, RED MIST

The battle-mist overcame Colum now. His knee lifted to drive into Donnan's crotch. As the man bent over in pain, Colum struck him a savage blow across the back of the neck with a closed fist. Donnan dropped like a felled ox and lay still.

But Colum wasn't done with him yet. Still cursing, he grabbed a fistful of red hair and raised Donnan's head, meaning to pound it into the ground.

Suddenly, it was Fergus he saw lying under him. This was no contest of champions. It was a blood-feud between the Ard-righ and himself—which could only end with the spilling of blood.

"Stop."

The word lashed Colum, piercing the red-mists that bound his mind. He lifted his head and saw a tall manshape from whose brow twelve-tined antlers sprung. The eyes that fixed their gaze on Colum were ageless, deep and knowing. Silently they spoke to him.

Would you break Fair-truce, Colum, Donal's son, and so be outlawed in truth?

The mist cleared from Colum's gaze—quickly and sudden, like the long grass of Kerry's plains parting before a storm wind.

THE FAIR IN EMAIN MACHA

THE TOR SF DOUBLES

A Meeting with Medusa/Green Mars, Arthur C. Clarke/Kim Stanley Robinson • Hardfought/Cascade Point, Greg Bear/Timothy Zahn • Born with the Dead/The Saliva Tree, Robert Silverberg/Brian W. Aldiss • Tango Charlie and Foxtrot Romeo/The Star Pit, John Varley/Samuel R. Delany • No Truce with Kings/Ship of Shadows, Poul Anderson/Fritz Leiber • Enemy Mine/Another Orphan, Barry B. Longyear/John Kessel • Screwtop/The Girl Who Was Plugged In, Vonda N. McIntyre/James Tiptree, Jr. • The Nemesis from Terra/Battle for the Stars, Leigh Brackett/Edmond Hamilton • The Ugly Little Boy/The [Widget], the [Wadget], and Boff, Isaac Asimov/Theodore Sturgeon • Sailing to Byzantium/Seven American Nights, Robert Silverberg/Gene Wolfe • Houston, Houston, Do You Read?/Souls, James Tiptree, Jr./Joanna Russ • He Who Shapes/The Infinity Box, Roger Zelazny/Kate Wilhelm • The Blind Geometer/The New Atlantis, Kim Stanley Robinson/Ursula K. Le Guin • The Saturn Game/Iceborn, Poul Anderson/Gregory Benford & Paul A. Carter • The Last Castle/Nightwings, Jack Vance/Robert Silverberg • The Color of Neanderthal Eyes/And Strange at Ecbatan the Trees, James Tiptree, Jr./Michael Bishop • Divide and Rule/The Sword of Rhiannon, L. Sprague de Camp/Leigh Brackett • In Another Country/Vintage Season, Robert Silverberg/C. L. Moore • Ill Met in Lankhmar/The Fair in Emain Macha, Fritz Leiber/Charles de Lint • The Pugnacious Peacemaker/The Wheels of If, Harry Turtledove/L. Sprague de Camp* • Home Is the Hangman/We, in Some Strange Power's Employ, Move on a Rigorous Line, Roger Zelazny/Samuel R. Delany* • Thieves' Carnival/The Jewel of Bas, Karen Haber/Leigh Brackett* • Riding the Torch/Tin Soldier, Norman Spinrad/Joan D. Vinge* • Elegy for Angels and Dogs/The Graveyard Heart, Walter Jon Williams/Roger Zelazny* • Fugue State/The Death of Doctor Island, John M. Ford/Gene Wolfe* • Press Enter ■ / Hawksbill Station, John Varley/Robert Silverberg* • Eye for Eye/The Tunesmith, Orson Scott Card/Lloyd Biggle, Jr.*

*forthcoming

CHARLES DE LINT

THE FAIR IN EMAIN MACHA

TOR
fantasy

A TOM DOHERTY ASSOCIATES BOOK
NEW YORK

THE FAIR IN EMAIN MACHA

An earlier version of *The Fair in Emain Macha* originally appeared in *Space & Time* #68, edited by Gorden Linzner; copyright © 1985 by Charles de Lint.

Grateful acknowledgment is made to Robin Williamson for permission to use a portion of ''Five Denials on Merlin's Grave'' from the book of the same title published by Pig's Whisker Music Press; copyright © 1979 by Robin Williamson. For further information on Robin Williamson's work, write to: Pig's Whisker Music Press, at P.O. Box 27522, Los Angeles, CA 90027; or at BCM 4797, London WC 1N 3XX, England.

A Tor Book
Published by Tom Doherty Associates, Inc.
49 West 24th Street
New York, N.Y. 10010

Cover art by Mel Grant

ISBN: 0-812-50821-1   Can. ISBN: 0-812-50820-3

First Tor edition: March 1990

Printed in the United States of America

0 9 8 7 6 5 4 3 2 1

AUTHOR'S NOTE

I came to the field of fantasy and science fiction through the back door, as it were—from an interest in folktales, myths and traditional music. Like many of us enthused with fantasy at the time, I read the classic writers: Tolkien, naturally enough, but also Morris, Dunsany, Cabell, Eddison, Peake and the like. And then somewhere along the line I ran headlong into the works of Robert E. Howard and Fritz Leiber.

I decided I wanted to write when I was about fifteen and used to fill notebooks with poetry. My first attempts at writing fiction were painful pastiches of Morris and Dunsany that I never submitted to publishers. Happily, I put the fiction aside and devoted my time to playing music and gaining some life experience (both of which I still try to do), thereby saving numerous editors the onerous task of trying to wade through all that naive scribbling.

Fiction writing again reared its head in the late seventies as I expanded upon and gave fuel to the pen and ink work of an artist friend of mine, John Charette. This time around, the stories were pastiches of Howard, Moorcock, Leiber. They were equally as painful as the earlier ones, but at least they had a sense of story and characterization about them and eventually I went on to try and find my own voice.

The story of Colum was the first in which I began to utilize the material that had drawn me into this field in the first place. It's set in an Ireland that never was, but much of its background and, certainly, its mythic resonances are woven from

that same cloth of folklore, myth and song that brought me here so long ago.

For that reason—principally, although there are others—this story retains a warm spot in my heart.

No creative person works in a vacuum; those who say they do are only kidding themselves. The source material can't often be easily traced back—by the creator of the work as much as by those who partake of it—but we all know, or should know, that we have debts to pay. There are many writers whom I've admired, for many different reasons. When I have the chance, I like to thank them for the pleasures and inspiration they've given me. That's easy to do when they are contemporaries; far more difficult when it comes to someone like de la Motte Fouque, for example, or Dickens.

Fritz Leiber is an author whose career has spanned decades. I've had the opportunity to speak to him once, only briefly, but I've had years to enjoy and appreciate his work. Sharing this double with him is a wonderful opportunity for me to thank him again—this time in public.

If you'd like to know why I consider him to be such an important writer, go pick yourself up a copy of *Conjure Wife*, *The Wanderer*, the more recent *The Ghost Light*, or any other of his many wonderful books, and see what I mean.

Or just turn this Tor Double over and lose yourself in Lankhmar where you'll find the prime lesson that Leiber taught us with his Fafhrd and Mouser series, which is, that heroic fantasy can be adventurous and entertaining, yet still explore the universal truths that the best practitioners of any creative endeavor are trying to illuminate with their work.

In the meantime, I offer to Fritz Leiber *The Fair in Emain Macha* as but a tiny portion of the thanks that I feel I owe him for those many wonderful hours of reading he's given me.

—Charles de Lint
Ottawa; Summer 1989

vi

This is the noble truth of the arising
of sorrow. It arises from craving,
which leads to rebirth. . . .

—from *The Pali Canon*;
   sacred scriptures of the Theraveda
   Buddhists (c. 500–c. 250 B.C.)

Above and below all weir
the Green Man makes his play. . . .

—Robin Williamson,
   from "Five Denials on Merlin's Grave"

<u>ONE</u>

Twilight fingered the sky with grey threads of cloud as the horseman stepped his mount from the wood. He skirted a jumble of rock, avoiding the trail that led down into the marshes, and made his way to the chalk cliff that lay ahead. From that vantage point he could look out over the Erse Sea, that body of water separating Aerin from the main body of the Grey Isles. His own kin called it Nial's Arm.

A frown twitched on his brow.

Kin. Best not to remember; impossible to forget.

He had no kin now.

Seven years ago, his father had led him into a King-breaking—a justified rebellion

that ended in failure, death its only reward. The horseman had been the sole survivor of that final battle. He was the last of his clan; an outlawed wolf of Aerin, alone on a foreign shore. And soon to be outlawed here as well.

The horseman sighed. He dismounted wearily, swinging his right leg across his mount's forequarters and dropping lightly to the ground. The grass, blades bowed low by the sea winds, was springy underfoot. He stood in the quiet for a moment, listening, grey eyes watching his back trail with a wary gaze until he was satisfied that he hadn't been followed. Only then did he drop the reins and continue on foot to the lip of the cliff. Left to its own devices, his mount nibbled contentedly at the salted grass.

Aerin, the man thought, looking westward. Do you remember me still?

Seven years was a long time.

He stood tall and straight-backed, one hand plucking at his mustache, the other loosely resting on his swordhilt. The links of his mail tunic caught the last rays of the sunset and made a glitter of its captured light; his hair was as red as the sun itself as it now sank seaward. His gaze fixed on the misted distance, hoarding thoughts behind his eyes.

He yearned for justice as a blind man yearns for sight. Yearned for justice, and

for a welcoming smile from his own Meave whom he had been forced to leave behind.

His frown deepened at the thought of her, for he could not think of Meave without recalling her sire as well: Fergus mac Coemgen, Ard-righ of Aerin; the unbroken King who'd had the horseman's father slain and set his King's Curse on the horseman himself. In the years since his exile, word had come from Aerin: How his father's rath was less than a memory, how the clan's fields were salted and barren now, how their cattle fattened the Ard-righ's herds, their great black bull—his father's pride—servicing the Ard-righ's weaker stock.

Men, women, and children had all been slain. In the duns of his people, in the raths of the Kings, not even the harpers kept alive the memory of his clan. Only he remained, Colum mac Donal, truly his father's son, for the father's hatred for the unbroken King still lay unchecked and simmering in the son's heart. But retribution remained beyond his grasp. He was an exile, a chieftain of Artor Foes-slayer, with three companies of horse under his banner, his own keep, more land and gold at hand than his own father had ever known, but he was no closer to vengeance now than when he'd first left Aerin, a lad of seventeen summers and green as the woods in spring.

Staring westward, watching the sun set behind the green isle that had once been his

home, he knew he had to dare Artor's anger and return. He had no choice. For all the honor he had earned under Artor's Bear banner, he was still an outlaw, still wore a King's Curse in the land his heart named home.

Who was the Bear to forbid his going?

During his seven years of exile he had faithfully served the Bear as Artor's banner was carried across the Grey Isles. Cymrn lay under its protection now, and Midstland. Kernow, Endland and Thumbria to the very borders of Alban. They named Artor the Pendragon in the duns and raths of his liegemen. Chief of chiefs, King of Kings. What Norseman did not fear the sound of his horse companies come a-riding? What brigand stole through the Great Wood and did not keep a wary watch for the Pendragon's men? The chiefs of every tribe except those in the Highlands bowed their knee to him.

They had won peace, Artor and his horse companies. What need was there for an Aerin wolf when the battles were all done? To which did he owe his fealty now—liege or homeland?

Colum knew which call was stronger.

He remembered an evening two nights past when he and Artor had been out to take the night air, standing together on the high battlements of Caeme Tor. The conversa-

tion had turned to Aerin and Colum had spoken of returning, but the Bear shook his head in response.

"No," he said.

His voice was quiet, but it cracked with an edge that would brook no argument. The Bear was used to commanding, and expected his commands to be obeyed. It could be no other way. But that night Aerin stirred strongly in Donal's son and a queer streak of feyness made him argue.

"The Norse have stopped their vikings for a full season," he said. "The tribes are quiet—even the Picta. The whole summer long I've been at nothing but drilling and training recruits."

Artor nodded in agreement, but said nothing. He looked away, across the green slopes below Caeme Tor that lay cloaked in darkness.

"Why do you deny me?" Colum asked. "I ask for leave—a season at the most. Not to be forsworn."

Artor turned to him again.

"We're not all fools here, Colum," he said finally. "Use the good common sense that Ullr gave you and think of what you are saying. You'd go to an isle where every man's hand is against you . . . to accomplish what? Revenge? All you'll gain in Aerin is your death.

"But—"

"Give me one more year to see that the

peace we worked so hard to win here holds
and then I'll sail with you myself."

Colum shook his head. The darkness hid
the bitterness in his eyes, if not that in his
voice.

"You said that last year, *and* the year before, and still we train troops in Caeme Tor
and I'm no closer to home than I ever was.
If you'd go, go now. Let me scout ahead of
you. There are still those loyal to Coinneach
mac Conan. Think of it, man. You'd be a
liberator."

"And I say it's still too soon," Artor replied. "If I left now the tribes would be
yammering at one another's throats within
a fortnight. We'd return liberators of Aerin
with the task to begin all over again at
home."

"But—"

"Ullr take you! Are you deaf? I've said
no."

They faced each other, veins throbbing in
their temples, fists clenched at their sides,
each willing the other to back down. Colum
found himself considering the sword
sheathed at his belt and was half minded to
draw it and damn the consequences, when
he realized what it was that he was contem-
plating. He dropped his gaze from the
Bear's, reason prevailing, the anger untem-
pered.

"Follow your own head," Artor said
softly, "and you'll be outlawed here as well

as in your homeland, mac Donal. I'll hound you from shore to shore and never give you a moment's pause."

Colum looked up as the Bear stalked away from him. He bit back further argument. Under his anger, sorrow ran like a wide river, for he knew what he must do; knew as well that neither Artor nor the threat of a second King's Curse would stop him now.

He had to forget that they had been friends, the Pendragon and he.

After this day, they could only be enemies.

On that western cliff top, Colum shook his head, remembering. Caeme Tor was behind him now and the King's Curse was on his head—or would be, as soon as he set foot to ship's deck. Before the word went out, he must be gone from these shores. He would miss the Bear and his other comrades, but they would have to make do with one another for their company from now on. Tam O'Linn and Garn of the Fens. Ancelin with whom Artor had at last settled the difference as to whose wife Gwenore was to be. The druid Myrddin.

He would miss them, but Aerin's call had the stronger pull now. It was as though his homeland had lain a geas upon him, a geas to return he could no longer set aside.

He returned to his horse, mounted and

rode down the narrow twisting trail that led, on one side, into the fens, on the other, to Clynnog-fawr sprawled along the coast below. There would be traders docked there, a passage across Nial's Arm that he could buy. He unrolled his cloak from behind his saddle as the night's chill deepened. It was a plain cloak, woven from wools dyed a muted green and blue. His scarlet cloak—that which marked him as one of the Pendragon's captains—lay rolled around his commander's torc in his keep near Caeme Tor.

He no longer had a need for either.

TWO

He sailed on the morning tide, the gulls haggling like fishwives overhead, the salt spray in his hair. Cymrn fell away behind him, but he looked only westward, waiting for his first glimpse of Aerin and her green shores.

He wondered vaguely at what course the Bear's anger would take. Would he sail to Aerin to reclaim his errant captain? The notion pulled a grim smile from Colum's lips. What dark humor that would be, if his desertion was what it took to influence Artor to cross Nial's Arm.

But mostly he let the past seven years slip away, just as the shores of the Grey Isles

slipped away behind the wake of the ship, and turned his mind to what lay ahead.

Was vengeance so important?

He remembered his father's face, features twisted in a death mask as he lay on the battlefield, and knew that, if nothing else, retribution was necessary for his father's sacrifice not to have been in vain. The harpers should be singing the great deeds of the Fiolan clan. When their songs told that Donal's son had set Coinneach mac Conan on his rightful throne, that a Fiolan had returned the High King's Seat to Temuir where it belonged, then the bitter taste of his clan's defeat would finally be washed away. They would be remembered with honor once more and their ghosts would finally know peace.

But what of Meave? Would she still be waiting?

Colum shook his head. There it was not such an easy thing to guess how it might end. He had sent no word—how could he? But seven years was a long time for silence. That he had taken no other woman to his bed during that time ... how was she to know? But if she would still have him ... there were the far western lands, across Atlanta, where his sister Aine had gone before the trouble began; to them, to Aerin Nua, he'd take Meave if she was willing. But first ...

He sighed.

The Fair in Emain Macha

First there was the small matter of who should sit in the High King's throne.

"Your thoughts seem heavy, for one who's returning home."

Colum turned at the voice. There was a man at the rail beside him, his features hidden in the hood of his brown cloak. Colum wondered at the man's silent approach, then gave a mental shrug. He'd been so lost in thought that a longship of Valkings could have come alongside the ship and he wouldn't have noticed them.

"Home," he said softly, looking west again.

He must have the look about him of a man returning. The way his gaze strained ahead into the distance. The sense of anticipation that hung over him like a bright cloak that could not possibly be missed.

"It's a long time since I've seen Aerin's shores," he added.

The man at his side murmured sympathetically. They stood at the rail silently for a while, gaining their sea-legs. The sun was warm on their faces, the salt spray cast up from the bow, invigorating. The rigging creaked as the sailors raised the ship's sails. The gulls continued to follow in its frothy wake, filling the air with their raucous cries.

"And what will you do when you arrive home—Colum mac Donal?" the stranger asked suddenly.

Colum stepped back from the rail, hand falling to the hilt of his sword.

"Who—?"

The stranger lifted back his hood and let it fall to his shoulders, revealing features browned by sun and rough weather. The man's long dark hair was tied back with a leather thong; his eyes were a startling pale blue when measured against his complexion and flickered with secret knowledge.

Colum knew those eyes, knew that face.

"Myrddin," he breathed.

His fingers tightened on his swordhilt and he took another step back.

"Has the Bear sent you to bring me back?"

The druid shook his head. A half smile touched his lips, then he looked away across the waters again as though nothing had interrupted their conversation.

"Who is Artor to command me?" he asked.

"Then why are you here, man?"

Myrddin was quiet for a long while. Finally he shrugged. When he spoke, his voice had a wistful note in it.

"Perhaps," he said, "to bid farewell to a friend too much in a hurry to come to me himself."

"Ah . . ."

Colum's voice trailed off and his wariness fell from him. He took his place beside the druid once more.

"And how could I, Myrddin?" he said. "How could I know that you wouldn't tell the Bear? He would have stopped me before ever I stepped through the gatehouse of Caeme Tor. I wouldn't willingly raise my sword against him, but . . ."

"And I?" Myrddin asked. "Could you raise it against me?"

Colum shook his head. "Of all men . . . I've heard the story often enough of how you argued with Artor to take me in when this same sea washed me ashore by your camp. It was an omen, you said then."

"It *was* an omen," the druid said. "And wasn't it fulfilled? The Isles are peaceful now and will you tell me that your hand was not in the making of that peace? But our work is done. The Bear can hold his land without our help now. It's time we went on to fulfill the destinies of our own lives."

Colum nodded thoughtfully. "And the Bear? You spoke to him of this?"

"I did."

"And he said?"

"You've his King's Curse upon you, Colum. He said he'd warned you it would come to this."

Colum made no reply, only stared at the waves.

"Surely you knew it would be so?" Myrddin said. "How could you expect the Bear to take back his word?"

"I knew," Colum replied softly. "It wasn't a . . . thing I desired. But I expected it. He warned me plainly enough."

"What will you do now?"

Colum sighed. "I'm bound for the rath of Coinneach mac Conan. And you?"

"I'd go with you—if you'll have my company."

Myrddin smiled at Colum's surprise.

"And why not?" the druid added. "Does the wolf disdain to travel with the fox?"

Colum grinned and shook his head. "Not this wolf. But why? Another omen?"

"Not as such. It's been years since I've walked the low green hills of Aerin. I've found myself wanting to hear her harpers and the sweet music of the Erse tongue once more. I grow tired of Cymrn, tired of Artor's brooding since he sent Gwenore off with Ancelin.

"Tired of war and the endless talk of war. . . ."

"Then you travel to the wrong isle," Colum said, his grin vanishing. "I mean to start a King-breaking in Aerin and I won't rest until I'm dead or the deed's done. You travel into war, Myrddin, not from it."

"War?" the druid repeated. "Perhaps. But is it war when only two men fight?"

"What do you mean?"

Myrddin shrugged. "Sometimes the words simply come—and not at my bid-

ding. But look, Colum. Isn't that the coast of Lagan that I see?"

Colum looked to the west. Rising from a bank of low-hung mist was a long streak of grey and green. Land. His homeland. As he looked upon it, all questions were forgotten.

"It is," he murmured.

A great joy settled in his heart. Trials lay ahead. Death crouched at his elbow, awaiting the harvest that was surely to come. But in this moment, Colum knew only that a part of him that had been lost had now been found once more.

"It is," he repeated. "It's Aerin we see. . . ."

THREE

They made landfall at Howth on the coast of Lagan, the easternmost of the five kingdoms of Aerin. From there they rode north to Temuir, Coinneach's rath. Once it had been the High King's Seat, the rath of the Ard-righ over all Aerin, but when Fergus took the throne, he moved the King's Seat to Emain Macha in Uloth, leaving Temuir deserted except for those of Coinneach's clan.

The man at the rath's gates stared with wide eyes at the pair when Colum named himself and his companion. He made the Sign of Horns, in case it was a shade of the dead that had come calling on his lord, but let them in, sending word into the rath of

who it was that had arrived. Only moments after the gates opened, Coinneach himself was there to greet them. Wordlessly, Lagan's King stepped forward and clasped Colum to his breast.

"It's been too long, Donal's son," Coinneach murmured. "Far too long since these eyes looked upon one of the Faolta. Though the dun of the Wolf lies open to the sky and its winds, though the King's Curse lies upon you and your clan, still you are welcome."

As they broke their embrace, Colum stared at this man—his father's friend and the rightful Ard-righ of Aerin. The years had not bowed Coinneach. Though now in his late fifties, he stood tall and straight as a young sapling, but with an old oak's strength in his limbs. His hair was black, his brow wide, and the gaze that met Colum's was as piercing a grey as Colum's own. Though Coinneach was recognized as a King—of Lagan still, if not all Aerin—he was simply clothed in leather leggings and a wool tunic, but his manner was generous, as befit an Erse King.

"Lord," Colum said respectfully and inclined his head.

He could say no more.

After Coinneach had been introduced to Myrddin, he called for retainers to stable their mounts. Then he took Colum's arm and led the two across the dirt courtyard and into the Mi-Cuarta, the great banquet-

ing hall of Temuir that was Coinneach's own dun.

Inside, there was room for two hundred men, though now it housed barely three score. It had a high roof with broad beams supporting its heavy timbers. The walls were wood as well, except for the stone foundation that was to a height of three feet. Long tables stretched the length of the hall, with sleeping cubicles along either wall. At the far end, on a low dais slightly above the rush-strewn floor, was Coinneach's own cubicle near the central hearth.

Lagan's King gave the two travelers the guest cup himself, then smiled as they sat to eat. A harper played, sitting on a stretched piece of speckled doe-skin near Coinneach's cubicle, and Colum listened to the man sing as he ate. The Erse lilt in the harper's voice and the strong mead—drawn from a vat near the door—brought home the fact that he had returned, truly returned, with far greater impact than setting foot at Howth had ever done. Even the venison had a subtle difference of flavor that set it apart from the meat of Cymrn and the rest of the Grey Isles.

When he could finally eat no more, he pushed his platter aside, cleaning his greasy fingers on his leggings.

"What news is there?" he asked, after waiting for the harper to complete the song

he was half singing, half chanting. "I've been away seven years with nothing but rumors and memories to feed my hunger."

Coinneach regarded him, a troubled look in his eyes.

"There's little new," he said. "Fergus still holds the throne and the land withers under his rule, but his position is strong and the druids can do nothing to remove him." He paused, then added, "Did you know your sister escaped to Aerin Nua?"

Colum nodded. "Has there been word from her?"

"None that we have heard."

"And what of Meave?" Colum asked.

"Who?"

At Coinneach's confusion, Colum realized the mistake he'd made. Meave was the name he would always know her by, but her father had named her otherwise.

"Triona," he said. "Fergus's daughter."

Coinneach gave him a shrewd look. "So it *was* you."

"What do you mean?"

"The harpers' songs tell how she went into the wilds with an outlaw, though there's not one man knows who he might be for she won't name him." Coinneach smiled. "You've a son, Colum. Did you know that?"

"A . . . son?"

Coinneach laughed. "Yes, a son. And now I understand the riddle of his name. She

Charles de Lint

called him Connal—named him for both
you and your father."

"Connal. . . ."

Colum stared into unseen distances, a
foolish grin spilling over his features. He
turned to Myrddin.

"Did you hear?" he asked. "A son!"

The druid smiled. "I heard, Wolf."

"Where is he?" Colum asked. "And his
mother. Mea—Triona. Where are they?"

A shadow crossed Coinneach's face.

"I don't know where your son is," he said
softly. "It enraged Fergus—not knowing
who the father was. He would have killed
the babe out of hand except that the druids
forbade it. They laid a geas on him that was
so strong not even Fergus could dare break
it."

"And?" Colum prompted. "Tell me, man.
What happened to him?"

"Beineon took the child to keep him safe
from Fergus. The tale is that he fostered the
boy with the sidhe. And, Colum . . . as for
Triona. Fergus chains her to the wall of his
Mi-Cuarta each night until she will name
the boy's father. He means to marry her off
to one of his Valking allies—a man named
Guttorm."

Colum's features tightened with anger.

He had a son, fostered by the sidhe? The
boy would be no more than six—if he still
lived.

20

And Meave. Chained in her father's hall. Married to a Norse. . . .

"No!" he cried. He pounded the table with his fist, sending mead mugs scattering to the floor. "How could no one stop it? Are the Erse all cowards?"

Coinneach's face darkened with his own anger.

"Talk as you will, Donal's son," he said. "But tell me this: Where were you these past seven years?"

"I? I'm but one man alone."

"And so is each one of us," Coinneach said. "And when have the clans gathered to a common cause except at the peace-swearing of the Fairs? When Muman's Fachtna is feuding with Oran over a cattle-raid three years past and gone, and Seanan—the wealthiest man in Connacht now—will not speak with his own King. . . . Do I need to go on?

"And even could the clans unite, the High King's Gailana are everywhere with Fergus's Valking allies at their side. The druids are silent and there's not a man in Aerin who will step forward now—not since the Faolta clan was defeated; their dun no more than a memory and their last son with the King's Curse on his head."

"But—"

Coinneach cut him off. "We work towards a King-breaking, but it's slow work. It takes time. I have men training, the

smiths are readying my war chariots, but I can't raise an army overnight—not even over seven years of nights. Not when I have my own borders to protect as well.

"The day will come when we will march on Uloth and take Fergus's throne, but it's not come yet."

Coinneach looked away, his sense of frustration bringing a dark bitterness to his eyes. In the silence that followed Coinneach's argument, the immediacy of Colum's anger ran from him. In its place burned a slow smoldering fire that he knew wouldn't die until he had Fergus's head hanging from his belt.

"How can I help?" he asked finally.

"The Fair," Coinneach replied. "The Great Fair in Emain Macha. I meet then with Muman's King. If I can win him to my banner, the others will follow his lead."

"And I? What is it you'd have me do?"

"Best his champion. Fachtna won't listen to me otherwise."

Colum nodded, understanding. He remembered his father speaking of Muman's King. Best him fairly and he would follow you ungrudgingly.

"And who is his champion?" Colum asked.

"Donnan mac Ailin," Coinneach replied.

"I don't know the man."

"He hasn't been beaten once," Coinneach

22

said. "Not in the four years since he became Muman's champion."

Colum slept little that night. He lay restlessly on the furs in his cubicle for long hours, thinking of a young woman with chestnut hair. A young woman as fair, in the eye of his memory, as any queen of the sidhe.

Meave.

Their time together had been short—a few weeks stolen in the aftermath of a Valking raid and the pair of them little more than children. She'd be a woman now, as he was a man. What did she think of Donal's son and the seven-year-long silence that lay between them?

Colum sat up. Taking his sword in hand, he laid its sheathed length across his knees.

Whatever she thought of him, he would win her her freedom. No Erse maid deserved to be wed to a Valking. He would see her free and then let her make her own choice. If gentle Angus Og thought to look kindly on them, perhaps, just perhaps, she would go away with him. Away from these isles. Away from wars and the bitterness of old griefs that haunted them.

They could sail to Aerin Nua. It wasn't Tir nan Og, to be sure, but a blest land still, if half the tales he'd heard of it were true. It was a place without Kings. A land of wide open plains and tall, forested mountains. A

land of promise and hope. Together they could go, and with them their young son. . . .

Connal.

A deep warmth stirred in Colum. He set aside his sword and stretched out on the furs once more.

Connal mac Colum.

He knew that it was more imperative than ever that he reclaim the honor that had once belonged to his clan's name. For how else could his son wear it with pride?

FOUR

Colum and Myrddin were with Coinneach mac Conan's party as it rode north to the Great Fair in Emain Macha on the following day. Colum wore the leaf-green livery of Lagan's King. Myrddin had dyed the Wolf's flame-bright red hair, mustache, and eyebrows a stark black. The simple change was so remarkable that his own horse company in Caeme Tor might well have had trouble recognizing him. His name was Seadna mac Fionntan now. Seadna, Fionntan's son, in the employ of Coinneach mac Conan, King of Lagan.

Myrddin wore the robes of an Erse druid—drab and brown, though decorated

with a subtle embroidery of red, gold and green thread. He carried a holly staff.

The company rode at an easy pace, across flat pastures, skirting the bogs and dark woods. On the morning of their third day, they came at last to the gentle hill lands of the north and finally, nestled in among them, Emain Macha. Colum scratched at his scalp—the dye was making his skin itch— and stared at the structures that dotted the hills before them.

He regarded the buildings and tents with mixed emotions.

Meave was there, but so was Fergus.

Patience, he told himself. But he had never been a patient man.

Fergus had patterned Emain Macha after the rath of Temuir. He had made use of the original twin stone towers that had stood there long before he was born and built around them. His Mi-Cuarta was all of wood and commanded the space between the towers. Outward from it spread the secondary halls: the houses for the lesser Kings; the Grianan, or sun-house, for their Queens; the Stronghold of the Hostages where Meave would be kept when she wasn't on display in the Mi-Cuarta; and the Star of the Bards. Farther outward still, spreading down the hill, were the halls of Fergus's retainers and the people of Emain Macha, while beyond them were a host of newer structures.

The Fair in Emain Macha

As they approached, Colum cursed when he realized that these latter buildings housed Fergus's Valking allies.

People from all across Aerin were camped around the hill, their tents and encampments extending to the slopes of its neighbors. Wherever Colum looked, he could see preparations being made for the Fair. There were cattle grazing between the tents, watched over by small bands of boys with staves in hand. Gaudy tents displayed crafts and wares. There were areas marked out for tests of strength and other contests. Everywhere was a bustle and flurry of people hurrying to make ready. But for all the holiday trappings of their clothes and gear, there seemed to be little happiness in the air—nothing like the Great Fairs that Colum remembered from when he was a boy.

Coinneach's company made their way through the crowds, aiming for the hall that had been set aside for Lagan's King and his people close by the Mi-Cuarta. Colum fretted in his saddle, straining hopefully for a glimpse of Meave, but fearing what he would do when he did see her. Could he hold in his rage? When he thought of her shame, chained in her father's hall, offered up to one of her father's Valking allies . . .

Guards in the deep yellow livery of Fergus's Gailana took their horses when they reached the Mi-Cuarta and escorted them

toward the hall. As they drew near its threshold, there was a sudden movement from inside and then Fergus was there.

He was dressed in a rich robe interlaced with gold wire and jeweled studs. There was a torc of gold about his neck and a girdle inlaid with precious stones at his waist. Armbands and rings glinted in the sunlight. But for all his finery, his coarse features belied his claims to the throne of the Ard-righ. His cheeks were heavy-jowled, his eyes small and gleaming, his hair thin and a plain brown. His figure was stocky—more a merchant's body than that of a warrior, or a High King of a race of warriors.

"Greeting, Coinneach," he said, stepping from the doorway. His voice had an oily, perfumed quality to it. "You are the last to arrive."

In his guise as an Erse druid, Myrddin regarded the Ard-righ dispassionately. How had such a man taken the throne? he asked himself. Taken it, and held it.

He glanced at Colum and saw the rage that was building up in his companion's face.

Not now, Myrddin thought.

The druid could understand Colum's wrath, but to allow it free rein at this time would only abort their plans and undoubtedly be the death of them all. There were too many Gailana about—armed and waiting on their King's slightest order.

With his hand at his side, hidden from the gaze of the Ard-righ, Myrddin made a small motion with his fingers. It went unnoticed by the Gailana and either of the Kings, but Colum felt the power of it work on him. His limbs froze and his face composed itself. The hand that had been inching towards his swordhilt fell limply to his side.

"You will be at the banquet this evening?" Fergus was saying.

Coinneach nodded in reply.

"Good. Perhaps afterwards we can take a walk together. I have much to speak of with you."

He turned aside, indicating that he was done speaking. Coinneach made a brusque bow, then led the way into his own hall. With Myrddin still controlling him, Colum felt his body fall into step with the others and enter it with them.

FIVE

Colum could easily have done without the banquet in Fergus's hall that night. Surrounded by what he could only consider his foes, he felt naked without the mail he usually wore. Coinneach hadn't allowed it because it would give him away as an outlander when he was supposed to be Seadna mac Fionntan, a Lagan man. Few Erse wore mail, or any armor, considering it unmanly to fight in it. Colum's father had scorned this when he went up against Fergus and Colum agreed with his father's thinking. Why give the foe an advantage?

But neither mail nor armor had helped the Faolta that day.

No, they had died to the man, except for

him, and sitting here, like a corpulent spider at the center of its web, was the man responsible. All Colum asked for was a few moments alone with the man. Then he'd—

Colum caught Myrddin watching him. With an effort, he put the thought away and concentrated on the hall and the people in it.

The men and women serving them wore plain brown tunics. They were unsmiling— but cowed, rather than unfriendly. There was no order to the seating this night, so harpers sat with shanachies, the files recited their poetry from where they sat with the warriors and the scholarly ollams. Only at the far end of the hall were men seated according to rank. There the Kings ate and drank with their Ard-righ, their captains and retinue near.

Colum had his anger better in check now, though it still threatened to break free at any moment. Again and again his gaze raked the hall, looking for Fergus's daughter who should have been chained to the great oaken central support by now. But tonight the oak post reached high to the rath's roof, unattended.

Where was she? Colum asked himself. Still in the Stronghold of the Hostages? Was Fergus being cautious in how he shamed her—here before the gathered Kings of Aerin? Or was it that she was betrothed

now and he mustn't lessen the worth of the gift she would make to his allies?

He lifted a hand to pull at his mustache, dropping it when he remembered the dye. He tapped his fingers on his thighs, tension building in his shoulder muscles. He could feel Myrddin's gaze on him, wary, watching.

Then finally the meal was done and Fergus took Coinneach aside. They left the hall to walk in the courtyard that encircled the MiCuarta, Fergus attended by two of his Gailana, Coinneach bringing Colum. Three yews grew in the shadow of one of the towers. Fergus paused when he reached them and sat on the stones under the boughs, motioning Coinneach to sit with him. Colum and the Gailana took up positions nearby.

"I know what your feelings are toward me," Fergus told Coinneach. "And yet I can forgive their treason, if you will stand with me tomorrow."

"I . . ."

"Guttorm comes then," Fergus went on before Coinneach could speak. "He arrives with three longships of warriors from the Norselands. When this Feis comes to its end, I mean to give him my daughter in marriage—to bind our friendship for all time."

"It's no secret what you mean to do," Coinneach replied, his anger only barely contained.

The Fair in Emain Macha

A few paces away, Colum's fingers clenched into fists.

No, he told himself. Listen. Wait. But ochone, it was hard.

"But do you know why?" Fergus was saying. "The Norse have always been our foes—is there a man in Aerin that ever questions this? We are two warrior peoples, forever at odds. Only think a minute. With them as our allies—Erse and Valking united—what could stand before us?

"We could take the Grey Isles, then move from them across to the mainland itself. Even Aerin Nua could be ours. It lies across Atlanta and calls itself free, but an iron hand could bring it as quickly to heel as we will soon bring Artor's people."

"What . . . has this to do with me?" Coinneach asked after a long moment of silence.

"I offer you this," Fergus replied. "Aid Guttorm and I in our endeavors and as soon as the Grey Isles have fallen and we begin our assault on the mainland, I will give you the High King's Seat to do with as you wish. You will be the Ard-righ—you must only swear on your word never to strike against us."

"My word."

Fergus nodded. "Your word is legendary, Coinneach. It will be enough."

"If you know that," Coinneach said, "then you know as well that I've sworn to overthrow you, once and for all."

"Yes," Fergus said. "Let us speak plainly. Do you think me blind, deaf and dumb? I've been aware of your plots and your plannings, but why would you set your countrymen at one another's throats when I offer you a way in which you may have this throne you covet so much, and be rid of me as well, *without* bloodshed?

"I have men loyal to me and, with my Norse allies, enough strength to hold this island under my rule for as long as I wish. But my ambitions are greater. To fulfill them I need your support. The other Kings will listen to you, Coinneach. They will never support your King-breaking, for no matter how much they hate me, their loyalty to the High King's Seat is stronger, even with myself on that throne. But if you swear peace, they will keep it with you."

"You can't send a front to attack the Grey Isles while dealing with a rebellion at home, can you?" Coinneach said thoughtfully.

"Exactly. So give me your answer, Coinneach mac Conan. Can you be patient a year or two longer, or must we have war here in your beloved green isle? Can you not swallow your pride for such a short time?"

Coinneach would not look at him. He lowered his gaze to his feet. Colum stepped closer so that he could hear Coinneach's reply. Fergus's plans were the grandiose raving of a madman and yet . . . and yet he could succeed. Not even the Bear with his

horse companies could hope to prevail against massive invasions on either coast.

"Your word is all I require," Fergus repeated.

Coinneach lifted his head.

"My word?" he said. His voice was hard and sharp as a blade's cutting edge. "My word's been given once. What honor would it retain if I were to take it back and then give it out again? Lugh show us some light!"

"Peace, Coinneach," Fergus murmured.

"How can there be peace? Speak plainly, you said, so I ask you this: How can you speak of sworn oaths, you who have never kept the one? Shall I sell my people as though I were a merchant? Ask them for peace yourself, High King. Speak before the people and let them give you their answer."

Tension thickened in the night air. Fergus's guards clapped hands to their sword-hilts and Colum watched them carefully with a narrowed gaze.

Had Fergus grown so mad that he would allow his men to break Fair-truce? he wondered.

But when Fergus spoke, his voice was soft—like a peddler's.

"Think upon it, Conan's son."

"I have thought upon it—for as many years as my hands have fingers." Coinneach's voice softened now, too. "Think, Fergus. Think of what you mean to do. Not even the druids will allow it. Remember

your daughter's child. This time the druids
will set such a geas upon you that—"

"The druids are mine to control!" Fergus
cried. "I do not ask—I command. Did you
think I cared for that child of my daughter's? The grub could choke on its own spit-
tle for all I cared. I obeyed the druids then
because it was *my* will to do. To show the
people that I still upheld the old ways. But
those ways are changing. The druids will
obey me in this—as will the people.

"I give you a chance, Coinneach. Do not
throw it away. How many of the Kings do
you think will come to your aid if my Norse
were to storm Temuir this winter?"

"Don't threaten my people," Coinneach
began, but Fergus overrode him.

"Concerned with their own lands and
their cattle, the hunting and the cleaning of
weapons. . . . Do you think the other Kings
will come to your aid when the winter's
deep and the roads are bound with mud? I
don't think so, Coinneach. Your dun would
be torn down around your ears and you in
it before they ever arrived—*if* they could
even agree to come in the first place."

"If it's war you want!" Coinneach cried,
leaping to his feet.

"It's war—but not with you."

They stood face-to-face, Coinneach tow-
ering over the Ard-righ, his face flushed
with anger; Fergus's jowls quivering, his
small eyes ferret-bright. Colum and the Gai-

lana stood uncertainly to one side, hands on their weapons, fearing a Truce-breaking or worse, but not one of them willing to make the first move until they knew that their respective King was truly in danger.

"No more," Fergus said. "Think on this, Coinneach, and give me your answer on the last day of the Feis."

"You have my answer now."

"And I will have it again then."

Coinneach glowered at him.

Fergus shook his head. "You should have a wife to temper your angers, Coinneach," he added. "A babe to bounce on your knee."

"I—"

Fergus lifted one hand imperiously. "Go drown your anger in ale," he said. "I won't hear another word of this until the Feis ends. Go."

Coinneach's shoulders shook with anger, his hands opening and closing at his sides. For a moment Colum thought Coinneach would strike the Ard-righ, but then he turned abruptly and strode away. Colum hurried after him, his head spinning with all he'd heard.

Coinneach was the one to caution patience, he thought with black humor. Just listen to him tonight.

But Colum knew as well as Lagan's King that time was running out for them. What else could Coinneach do but speak plainly?

They returned to the hall set aside for

them without speaking to each other. Silence hung the length of the building, long and brooding as Coinneach paced back and forth. When he finally paused and spoke to Colum, his voice was calm again, but edged with iron.

"The lesser contests are tomorrow," he said. "Watch them. Fill your head with them. But guard your strength for on the day after, you meet Fachtna's champion and him you must beat. With Muman's King beside us, the others will listen to me."

"You'll go to war?" Colum asked.

"No."

Coinneach stared into the fire, his face an expressionless mask.

"Not war," he said. "It will be a King-breaking. But I don't doubt that the Morrigan's ravens will still feed their fill on the flesh of too many of Aerin's sons."

SIX

Colum and Myrddin wandered the Fair-grounds the next day, pausing to watch the various foot and chariot races, spear-throwing, sword play, foot races and wrestling acrobatics; noting the wealth that changed hands as the chiefs and their warriors wagered on the various outcomes. The bustle and confusion of the Feis surrounded them, no matter which way they turned. There were voices raised high in laughter. Fiddling, piping and harping. Songs sung, poems told, genealogies recited. In the stone circle on the hilltop above the rath where at Beltaine the summer fires burned high, a day-long moot was in its sixth hour. Below, in the farmer's

mart, men hired out and cattle were traded or sold. Hawkers cried their wares, selling ale and mead and whiskey, venison and boar's meat, cakes and breads.

Though they kept to themselves, they were still greeted by many, for at Fair-time, there were no strangers. Near the foot races, Colum met the King of Muman's champion. Donnan mac Ailin was a tall, wide-shouldered man with a wild thatch of red hair and a grin as broad as his face. He measured Colum with a keen gaze, for he knew that they would be rivals tomorrow, then he laughed. Thrusting a large tankard of ale into Colum's hand, he clapped the Wolf on his shoulder.

"Drink up, Seadna," he said, "for tomorrow's not today."

Colum smiled as he took the ale. Here was a man. Big as life, like the heroes of old, with a generous heart and a laugh like spring waters tumbling from the wintered hills. Tomorrow they would compete, but today they could be friends.

This, embodied in the one man, was the Aerin that Colum remembered.

They spied Fergus twice in the crowd.

The first time was when Colum was disengaging himself from a young Connacht woman with ale-merry eyes. The Ard-righ smiled at him as the woman ruffled Colum's hair for proving to be such a poor sport. Colum nodded to the High King, then

turned to watch a new foot race begin as the woman sauntered away, so he never saw her look at her hands and the black marks on them. She lifted a finger to her lips and tasted the dye, then laughed and wandered off.

But Fergus was watching her and he recognized the dye as well without needing a taste. Thoughtfully, he studied Colum for a time before moving on through the crowd.

The second time Colum noticed the High King was near a harping contest. Colum lifted his gaze from the red and silver strings of one harper's instrument to find Fergus watching him from the back of the crowd. When the Ard-righ saw that he was marked, he smiled and lifted a hand in greeting before walking off.

"He troubles me, that man," Myrddin said in a low voice.

"Small wonder," Colum said. "He's little loved and he knows it. He troubles everyone."

Myrddin frowned. "It goes deeper than that."

His gaze took on a far-off look, as though he saw into distances that lay far beyond the Fair at hand.

Colum touched his arm.

"Somhairle," he said, calling the druid by the Erse name he'd taken in Temuir.

Myrddin blinked. His gaze settled on Colum.

"Who is Beineon?" he asked. "Is he here?"

Beineon, Colum thought. Who'd fostered his son to the sidhe.

"He was my father's harper. Coinneach told us of him—remember?" Colum took the druid's arm, fingers tightening. "What did you see?" he asked. "Connal. My son. Is he . . . ?"

"Fine—so far as I know. But I've an uneasy feeling gnawing at my bones. Under all the humors of this Fair, I can feel an anger brooding . . . an anger that is more than the discontent of your people. I think it would be best if we found your son now, while we still have the time, rather than leave it for later when we might all be fleeing for our lives."

Colum's heart leapt at the thought. To see his son . . .

"But we agreed it was better to wait," he said reluctantly. "And you argued the loudest. . . ."

Myrddin nodded. "And now I counsel otherwise. I worried about Wodan's priests— the Norse druids that Guttorm will bring with him, but thought we could contain their mischief. Only now . . . now I can feel the land stirring restlessly under my feet, Wolf. This isle of yours is bound to its own laws—laws with which I'm not familiar. Tell me, what would happen if there was a peace-breaking at the Fair?"

The Fair in Emain Macha

"Why, the men would rise," Colum said. "The peace-breaker would be slain, his land salted. But . . . it's been longer than three of my own lifetimes since the Fair-truce has been broken. Who would dare?"

"Fergus?" Myrddin asked. "Or . . . When were there ever Norse at a Fair in Aerin?"

Colum nodded. Guttorm's men arrived today. There were other Norse in the houses beyond the rath of Emain Macha, though so far during the Fair they had kept to themselves. He had yet to see one of them. But today, when Guttorm arrived . . . How could Fergus keep his prospective son-in-law from joining the festivities of the Feis? And what would the Erse gathered here have to say to that?

Fergus trod a thinner line than perhaps even he realized, Colum thought. Sure disaster lay on either side.

"Beineon's an old man now," Colum said finally. "Since he's not here to judge the harping, I'd guess he would be in the Star of the Bards. Do you know the building?"

Myrddin nodded. "I saw it when we rode in. I think it's time I find out what I can concerning your son's fostering." As Colum rose to join him, Myrddin waved him back. "I'll go alone," he added. "Depending on what I learn, I might need to travel."

"I can—"

"You have to stay," Myrddin said. "Tomorrow you meet Donnan."

"But my son . . ."

"If you'd live to know him, you'll stay. Let me go, Wolf. Alone."

Colum glared at the druid. The child was his. Surely he was the one who should collect the boy from his fostering?

"You know this is how it must be," Myrddin said, as though reading his mind.

Colum nodded glumly. Reason won out, for all that his heart called him a fool. He knew that the fault lay with Fergus, not Myrddin. Fergus. The anger that smoldered in his chest awoke to flames, bringing a red mist to his eyes. If he could have that fat neck between his hands—

"Colum."

When Myrddin spoke his true name he seemed to hear it with his mind more than his ears. The word stole softly into his thoughts, delicate as a doe's footstep. But it was enough to cut through the red mist. He blinked to find Myrddin watching him, the blue eyes hooded.

"Keep a rein on that anger," Myrddin warned. "Your battle madness won't serve you well in this situation."

Do you think I can call it up or send it away at will? Colum wanted to ask the druid, but Myrddin had already turned away and disappeared into the crowd.

Frustrated, Colum returned his attention to the harping contest, but it no longer held any interest for him. He no longer cared for

it or any of the Fair's festivities, underlain as they were with a hollow gaiety. Instead, he made his way back to Coinneach's hall, the dull anger still sparking inside him for all that he worked to keep it under control.

It will come, he promised the fires inside him. Our time must come.

That afternoon Guttorm arrived with three hundred men. They were housed with the other Norse in their halls on the hillsides north and east of the Mi-Cuarta. And that night in the great hall, seven years fell away from Colum for once again he looked on his lost love Meave as she was brought from the Stronghold of the Hostages to meet her husband-to-be.

She was as beautiful as he remembered— perhaps more so. Her auburn hair gleamed in the torchlight, her amber eyes glittered. She held her head high and proud as befit an Erse princess. But Colum could see the despair locked behind her cool gaze. And when Guttorm approached her, he saw her shrink back from the man—the movement so imperceptible that he didn't doubt that he was the only one to see it, and that only because he looked for it.

Colum had dreamed countless times of this day when he would finally see her again, but he could never have imagined the moment to be so bereft of joy. His hand dropped to the hilt of his dagger as he

stared at her chains. His shoulders trembled. The red mist came to his eyes so that everything in the hall was turned to the color of blood in his sight.

He tried to fight the rage. He ground his teeth together, but the blood was drumming in his temples, making it impossible to think clearly. All he saw was Meave. Her chains and her torment. Then and there he would have attacked the Ard-righ, armed with only his dagger, if Coinneach had not laid a strong hand on his arm and pried his fingers from around the hilt of his knife.

"Peace," Lagan's King murmured. "Now is not the time."

Coinneach's warning by itself would not have been enough. But under his voice, Colum heard Myrddin speaking to him. His anger dulled to a coldness that settled like a stone in his stomach. The red battle-mist faded.

Carefully, Colum laid his hands on the table before him and looked around the room. No one had noticed him. All gazes were on the Norse King.

Guttorm had lifted Meave by the waist, his two huge hands easily spanning her narrow girth. Holding her up, he stood in place but made a slow circle, showing her off for all to see. The silence of the gathered Erse brought a grin to the Norse King's lips. His own warriors pounded their drinking mugs against the wooden table and shouted en-

couragements to their King. Setting Meave down, Guttorm hoisted a huge flagon of ale. Crying a toast to his bride-to-be, he downed the ale in one gulp, then threw back his head and laughed for the pure joy of the moment.

Not an Erse in the Mi-Cuarta could miss the man's mockery of them. They looked to their Ard-righ, but there was a cold look in Fergus's eyes that would brook no defiance of his will.

Colum couldn't turn his gaze to the High King himself—that was asking too much of the hard-won restraint that he could barely maintain. Instead, he watched Guttorm, marking the man for weaknesses and finding none.

He was a huge man, a half foot shy of seven feet. His hair was yellow and hung down his back in a long twist of a braid; his beard was tangled and dirty. Under his sheepskin vest, corded muscles rippled with every movement. Incongruous to his ragged clothing were his armbands of solid gold and the chains hung heavy with precious stones that dangled from around his neck.

He removed one of the latter and slipped it over Meave's neck.

"So!" he bellowed. "So do I name you Guttorm's bride."

His Erse was accented with the coarseness of his own tongue—making a mockery

of the language as he made a mockery of its people. Despair sped through Colum again as he watched Meave's gaze rake the hall, searching for one man to stand up to her father and redeem the honor of their people.

Her gaze traveled from face to face, finding only shame, but no aid. Men muttered and looked away—some unwilling, some unable to face her reproach.

And then her gaze found Colum's face and he knew that she recognized him for all his dyed hair and mustache and the years that lay between them. Her eyes went wide with surprise, then she narrowed her gaze and looked away.

Did hope rise in her heart to see him here? Colum wondered, his own heart aching for her. Or was it the final insult to her shame that he too should be present at this luckless moment?

As she composed herself again as best she could, Colum surreptitiously looked about the hall, but no one appeared to have noticed her momentary surprise. He began to relax, only to find that the Ard-righ was studying him, eyes narrowed in thought.

Was he remembering another face? Colum wondered nervously. Did Fergus recognize the blood of a Faolta warrior in Colum's features?

Fergus leaned forward in his seat.

"My daughter was ever the errant child," he said conversationally.

An expectant quiet settled over the hall. Meave gave her father a worried look that Colum knew mirrored the one that his own features wore.

"She was forever running off," Fergus went on. He smiled and shrugged his shoulders as if to say, what can you do? "I remember the day my counselor Ludgaidh brought her back from her latest and last escapade—I believe it was about the time of my Gailana's victory over the Wolf clan. He told me that she'd been in the company of an outlaw when he finally tracked her down, but she would never give up the man's name."

He knows, Colum thought. He glanced at Coinneach and saw understanding dawn on Lagan's King as well. They were discovered and there was nothing they could do about it—not surrounded by Fergus's Gailana as they were—but Colum edged his hand towards the knife sheathed at his belt all the same.

He would not go down without a fight.

"There was one body not accounted for when the Faolta were slain," Fergus was saying. "Donal's son, the young Colum. Now I find myself wondering: What if he and this outlaw were one and the same?"

A questioning murmur rose up in the hall

as the men considered their Ard-righ's words. Colum regarded Coinneach with bleak eyes, his fingers firmly gripped around the hilt of his dagger now. If he rose now and cast it at the High King . . .

Coinneach slowly shook his head. Do nothing, his eyes commanded Colum. Myrddin's voice whispered in Colum's mind in counterpoint to Coinneach's order.

Keep a rein on that anger. . . .

It took the greatest effort of will for Colum to force back the red mists and obey.

"It doesn't matter to me who she was with or when," Guttorm said, misreading Fergus's reason for bringing the matter up. "She won't have known a man until she lies with a Valking."

The murmuring in the hall took an ugly tone at the insult.

Fergus shook his head. "That's between you and your bride," he said. "The question I have now is: What if this same outlaw were here—in this rath—seated among us like a kinsman when the King's Curse is on his head?"

Men looked at those with whom they shared their tables, then sent their gazes farther through the hall to study their neighbors.

A Faolta? they asked. Here? Which of us . . . ?

Fergus rose to his feet and pointed at Colum.

"My Gailana," he cried. "The King's Curse is on that man—Colum mac Donal. I want him dead!"

A chaos of noise exploded in the Mi-Cuarta.

"Seadna is—"

"Faolta."

"Donal's son."

"Wolf clan."

"Lagan's champion."

The only swords in the Mi-Cuarta were those of the High King's guards. At his command, they moved forward, steel bared in their hands, but Coinneach rose to block their approach, his own followers and kinsmen holding Colum back as the brawny Erse struggled to meet the Gailana's attack.

"Would you break Fair-truce, Fergus mac Coemgen?" Lagan's King roared above the din.

"There is no peace in Aerin for the Faolta, Coinneach mac Conan," Fergus shouted back. He glared at his Gailana. "Why do you hesitate? I am your King. Kill the man!"

But there were others in the hall protesting now. It didn't matter to them that Colum had the King's Curse on his head. There was Fair-truce. There was honor. Donnan, the champion that Colum was to have faced tomorrow, drew his own short dagger and ranged himself beside Coinneach. Joining them a moment later was his

own King, Fachtna, and the Kings of Kerry and Uloth. And then, tall and thin as an old battered pine, the grey-bearded Ghabhann, chief of the druids, arose from his seat to face the Ard-righ.

"No man of Aerin shall break Fair-truce," he said, his voice cutting across the noise in the hall. "Be he Ard-righ or a warrior of the lowest rank."

The chief druid's voice seemed to echo on in the silence that followed his dictate. His too-bright eyes stared down the Gailana, one by one.

Guttorm turned to Fergus, a grin on his lips.

"There's no Erse blood in my veins," he said.

Fergus shook his head. He could see all too well that to kill Colum now would lead to a Druid's Curse falling on his own head and for all his arguments with Coinneach, that was a thing which he couldn't afford at this time. He still needed Aerin. When the Grey Isles fell and he had the head of Artor Foes-slayer on a spear before his tent . . . when his ships were turning toward the mainland . . . then . . .

"Chain him," he said. "Bind him in chains and take him to the Stronghold of the Hostages. And then, when the Feis is ended, we will see to it that King's justice is done. Will that suit you, Ghabhann?"

The Fair in Emain Macha

The chief druid nodded, plainly unhappy. Fair-truce gave freedom to all, outlawed or not, but to argue the point now would only lose them what they had gained. But the thoughts that ran through Ghabhann's mind lay all too plainly on the chief druid's face.

The Ard-righ grew too confident in his power. His gaze turned from the old gods and the old ways and only Lugh alone knew what the future held for Aerin with one such as Fergus mac Coemgen as its High King. But now was not the time, nor the place, for such considerations.

He stood aside, as did Donnan and then Coinneach and the other Kings. The Gailana pulled Colum's dagger from his hands and tossed it to the rush-strewn floor. They tore the colors of Lagan's King from his shoulders, then bound him hand and foot. Trussed like a raider's captive, he was carried from the Mi-Cuarta to the Stronghold of the Hostages.

Behind in the hall, the talk roared anew as men discussed who he was and why he'd come. The gazes of many men turned to Coinneach, speculation plain in their eyes. On the High King's dais, Fergus sat sourly nursing his ale. He looked out at his people and saw all too well how sentiment was running. Only the Norse were unconcerned, calling for more ale from the servitors as

though there had been no interruption in the festivities.

On the dais with her husband-to-be and father, Meave sat silent, staring at the door through which Colum had been taken. She said not a word, gave no sign of the anguish that stormed inside her.

SEVEN

Near midnight, as Fergus's Gailana were carrying Colum into the Stronghold of the Hostages in Emain Macha, Myrddin arrived at the dun of the Muireagain sidhe some leagues distant from the High King's Seat. He came in the robes of an Erse druid, with a holly staff in hand, but to the hidden gazes that watched him, it was the ancient strength and wisdom of an oak, hung with mistletoe, that gleamed in his eyes.

In front of the green knowe that housed the tulman of the sidhe, Myrddin tapped the staff on the packed earth at his feet. He called out a summoning word, then waited. The moon was full and rearing high in the

sky, shedding its brightness of its borrowed light across the hills.

And the sidhe were near.

He could feel the weight of their many gazes on him, watching him from all sides. He could smell the apple scent that followed them where they walked. He heard the sly rustlings and soft paddings of their light-stepping feet. They moved liquid as water. When they finally stepped out into the moonlight, it was as though shadows flowed from the deeper darkness where they had been hidden.

Myrddin stood, as silent as the moonlight, and regarded the gathered host. A good twenty of them surrounded him; there were more still hidden in the shadows.

They were the younger cousins of the Tuatha de Dannan and the Aelden of Artor's Isle. They reminded Myrddin of the Picta in northern Alban, for like the Picta, the sidhe were hill dwellers, too—slender and brown-skinned, with cloaks of fur and flint knives stuck in their belts, armbands and torcs of gold glittering bright. Bone arrows, feathered and flint-tipped, were notched in the gut strings of their yew bows.

"So," said one after silence had stretched between them long enough for the moon to have moved from the tip of one branch to the tip of another. "You've come."

"You know me?" Myrddin asked.

The sidhe stepped closer. His eyes were

a dark unreadable glimmer that burned and flickered like wind-caught leaves, wheeling and spinning. They were eyes a mortal could lose himself in. Myrddin matched him gaze for gaze, letting the little man drink deeply from the druid blue of his own gaze.

"Myrddin," the sidhe said. "The Fox-without-a-home. We know you."

"And do you know why I've come?"

The small head bobbed. "For the bairn. You've come for our fosterling, haven't you, Old One?"

"His father sends me," Myrddin replied.

Bowstrings slackened in the moonlight. The sidhe spokesman nodded wisely.

"So. Has the time come so soon? Has the long wait ended? Will Morrigan's ravens feed at last upon the not-King's body?"

Myrddin nodded. "Men will die. Many. But more not born of Aerin, than her own sons."

"And the not-King? Will he die?"

"He especially."

"And you?" the sidhe asked. "You of the Grey Isles, the Pendragon's druid. What is it that brings the Fox a-running to our door? The bairn alone?"

"Peace," Myrddin replied in a soft voice. "I seek peace."

The sidhe eyed him strangely. He seemed about to speak, then paused.

"It will be my final gift to the Bear," Myrddin explained. "He's fought for a long

time, always striving in the name of peace. Now that he has found a certain measure of it, I would not see a new war laid upon him—and war there will be unless Fergus the non-King is stopped."

"Your Bear will still die in battle," the sidhe said.

"I know. But not soon. Not at the hand of Fergus's Gailana, nor at the hands of his Norse allies."

"No," the sidhe agreed. "He will die at the hand of his own—"

Myrddin held up a hand and the sidhe fell silent, his prevision unspoken.

"The more we give voice to such prophecies," Myrddin began.

The sidhe nodded. "The more likelihood there is that they will come about. But some futures lie embedded in the very bones of the world, druid. We can no more change them than we can the course of the stars."

"I would wish him at least a fighting chance in avoiding his fate," Myrddin said.

The sidhe shrugged. A tiny woman approached them, leading a boy of six summers by the hand. Myrddin took in the red-brown hair and the features that were those of a man he named friend, except that they were softened by youth in the boy's face. The woman placed the boy's hand in Myrddin's, then stepped back.

"Lugh's luck go with you," the sidhe

spokesman said. "For it's that you'll need and more."

And then they were gone, the whole small host of them, vanishing as though the hill itself had swallowed them.

And so it had, Myrddin thought. They were all gone underhill. Safe in their tulman—the hollowed hill that was their dun. Safe underground while the war-birds flew overhead and Morrigan's ravens feasted.

The druid sighed. And then he remembered the look on the sidhe's face—that moment when he would have spoken, but forbore.

"What did they name you?" he asked the boy. "What was your sidhe-name?"

"Siochain."

Siochain. Peace.

"Were they so sure, then, that I was the one who would come?" Myrddin murmured, thinking aloud. "Did they know what I sought and for that reason named you as they did?"

"What do you mean?" the boy asked.

Myrddin shook his head. "Nothing, Connal-Siochain. Everything."

He looked eastward, then back at the boy.

"Do you want to meet your father and mother?" he asked.

"Oh, yes."

"Then we should be going now. The way's long for legs as short as your own."

* * *

Myrddin set an easy pace—not so quick that his young ward could not keep up, but steady enough so that the hills wound away underfoot and they continued to put a good distance between themselves and the dun of the sidhe.

Aerin's old rounded hills made the travel easy, if one kept to the ridges. The boreens were choked with undergrowth where the land was wild; where it was cultivated, there were the farmers' duns to be avoided. Tonight Myrddin had no desire to meet with any man—Aerin-born or not—for it was Colum's son he had in his care and he considered the boy's safety a great trust.

Reared among the sidhe, Connal was hardier than a mortal boy his own age would be. He kept up the steady pace, without complaint, but eventually his young legs grew tired and he began to lag. Myrddin carried him then, bearing the boy lightly for all the thinness of his own limbs, as though Connal had no weight to him at all.

They traveled in silence. Myrddin could not begin to guess his ward's thoughts, but he found his own turning more and more to the night itself, to Aerin and the feyness that seemed to ride her very air tonight. He sensed the approach of great deeds, the movement of gods, the presence of lesser deities. Once he thought he heard the baying of wolves and the winding of the Ant-

lered Lord's horn—distant, but close-sounding as well.

It was like faring abroad on Samhain night, he realized, when all the denizens of the Middle Kingdom were awake and walking the starlit hours between dusk and dawn. The air was charged with other-worldliness, familiar . . . and that which was less comfortably so.

For the druid sensed something else at that moment.

A tenseness crept across his shoulder blades. It warned him to be as cunning as his namesake, the fox. He smelled the sea in the air—a sudden sharp scent that stung his nose with its salty bite. He paused, lifting his head, his nostrils flaring as he read the wind. He searched the dark hills with a druid's gaze—before, behind, and around.

They were near their goal now. He could see the woods that bounded Emain Macha in the near distance. But closer . . . there was the sea . . . and something . . .

When the attack came, he was prepared for it.

But not enough.

He'd expected men and readied his magical arts to meet them. He'd set Connal down and called up the grey-gold flames of his magefire so that it blossomed from his palms. But he never had a chance to speak the sending words, nor cast the magefire at his enemies.

Invisible bonds trapped his mouth and arms—bonds as magical as any he himself could raise. They were the making of more than one mind and too strong for him to cast off. He delved deep inside himself, reaching for the strengths that were bound to the wild places of his soul, but he was too late. The enchantment that bound writhed and snaked through his mind, robbing his strength and making clear thought impossible. He was trapped, like a fox by the hounds, and he could do nothing when the yellow-haired Norsemen came out of the shadows towards him.

Nothing but rage.

Beside him, he could sense Connal's confusion and fear.

Flee, he willed at the youth, but the boy seemed to be caught by the same magical bonds that entrapped himself.

The Norsemen stepped steadily nearer, their yellow braids bouncing on the boiled leather of their armor, starlight glinting on their bared weapons—axe and sword. And then, behind the warriors, Myrddin saw the cause of his own helplessness: three Norse druids, priests of Wodan.

At the sight of them, he finally recognized the one-eyed god's touch in the magical fetters that held him. A cold icy breath of northern wind touched his cheek at their approach; a wind that Aerin's green hills never knew, not even in the dead of winter.

And then, their appearance striking him like the torch that lit the grave fire, he saw men of the Ard-righ's household walking among the Norse. By their presence, he knew they were truly undone. Fergus's Gailana would not be here unless they had already seen through Colum's disguise. So they were all the Ard-righ's captives now—Wolf and druid, the boy . . . and Meave, the boy's mother.

They'd been fools, Myrddin realized, and he the greatest one of all—walking the hills as though there was nothing in the world but fair men and justice.

How could he have been so blind?

He could see the strain on the faces of the Norse druids as they worked to hold him captive. That was enough to make him redouble his own attempts to wrest free of their influence, but strive though he did, he couldn't break the enchantment by which they held him. They were too strong and there was no more strength for him to call on.

This green isle wasn't his land. His magics drew their potency from the Grey Isles of the Bear, from the roots of its hills and its longstones, from Ullr and the Horned Huntsman, the Green Man of the Woods. They were kin to Aerin's gods, and so he could borrow strength from the land underfoot, but he couldn't borrow enough to defeat these three priests.

There was seawater in the flasks at their belts and stones from their cold home shores hung from leather thongs at their necks. Their foresight had given them their superior strength—a foresight that had eluded Myrddin when he sailed here with Colum a few short days ago.

Again he cursed his folly. If he had only thought to bring a handful of his own native earth with him. A few grains was all he would need to focus the attention of his own gods upon him.

The last thing he saw was the flash of a spear butt as it darted towards his head. It struck his temple with a sharp crack and then the darkness came to swallow him.

Oh, Colum, he thought as his consciousness ebbed away. Forgive me for failing you. . . .

EIGHT

As Colum brooded in the darkness of his cell in the Stronghold of the Hostages, the years fell away in his memory. Seven years ago he'd been jailed as well, waiting on the King's justice. But he'd been young then, with a youth's ability to hope. Youth rarely perceives its own mortality; this time he knew all too well what lay in store for him at the end of the Feis. He was trapped like a badger in its sett, bolt holes blocked and the smoke wreathing down the tunnels towards him.

His chance to redeem his clan's honor had been stolen from him.

His father's shade would never know peace.

Meave was bound for a Valking's bed.

Their son was condemned to bear his clan's shame.

For there was no escape.

He was chained and guards stood watch beyond the stout wooden door that barred him from freedom—yellow-liveried Gailana and yellow-haired Norseman. And beyond them, in his hall, was the High King Fergus, celebrating Colum's capture, no doubt, and his alliance to the piss-haired Norse that was partly won on the bartering of his own daughter's body.

Colum ground his teeth in helpless rage. When the red mist rose to cloud his sight, he let it come. There was no Coinneach to softspeak him to calmness. No druid to bind his limbs with enchantment. He let his anger dwell on the Ard-righ. On how, when they finally dragged him forth from his cell at Fair's end, he would, chains or no chains, bound or not, find some way to take Fergus with him to meet the Antlered God in his realm of death and reborning.

The red mist deepened across his gaze. His blood thrummed with useless rage.

At a sound that came from behind the door to his cell, he dragged himself to his feet. He struggled against the binding chains and gathered up as much of their slack as he could to strike out at his enemies. But when the door swung open, there

were no Gailana standing in its threshold. No Norse.

Colum blinked through the red mist. He saw Coinneach and Muman's King, Fachtna. Beside Fachtna was red-haired Donnan, Muman's champion. Behind them were others of Coinneach's clan and men he couldn't recognize because they were in shadow.

It's a glamor, Colum realized. Sent to confuse me.

He gathered the chains more tightly in his fists, bunching his shoulder muscles as the man who wore Coinneach's face took a step closer.

"Colum," the illusion said in a hoarse whisper. "Have you gone mad? We're friends, man—come to free you."

Colum shook his head as the words fought their way through his mist-clouded mind.

Friends, were they? Then why did they have weapons bared in their fists. Why . . .

But then his gaze dropped to the ground behind the illusions where he saw the head and shoulders of a Norse guard. Neither was connected to the other.

Colum looked up to study the King of Lagan's features, blurry as they were in the red cloud of his vision.

"Coinneach . . . ?"

At the King's nod, the red mist faded in Colum's vision. He staggered and Coin-

neach caught him before he could fall. Other hands steadied him while Coinneach unlocked his chains and then the night skies of Aerin were above him, Brigit's stars glittering and gleaming in their dark sea.

"Softly now," Donnan said.

He was supporting Colum on his right side.

Colum nodded and stepped free from the man's grip. The red mist was gone. His anger remained, but it was no longer a berserker's unthinking rage. It was cold now—fierce and bitter as only a winter wolf's can be.

As he was led from the Stronghold of the Hostages, through Fergus's rath and to freedom, the circulation returned to his arms and legs. By the time they were slipping through the camps surrounding Emain Macha, he felt fit enough again to do what he knew must be done. He stopped when only Uloth's green hills surrounded them, boreens cutting between them, the woods dark in the starlight.

"No farther," he said. "You've my heartfelt thanks for freeing me, but now you lead me away from where I must go."

"But, Colum," Coinneach began.

"No. I won't be ruled in this. What comes next lies between Fergus and myself. Blood cries out to be spilled—for the wrongs done to my father and kin, for the wrongs done to Meave and my son, for the wrongs done to

me. I won't listen to any more talk of waiting, Coinneach mac Conan. You, yourself, it was who asked me what I have done to right those wrongs in the seven years of my exile and I answered you, nothing. But I will right them now—in the Ard-righ's blood—and damn the consequences."

Coinneach faced him, not giving back an inch to Colum's anger.

"And you will listen to me, Colum mac Donal," he said. "It wasn't to spill blood that we rescued you. The Fair-truce still holds and—"

"Fair-truce? Then whose blood drips from your blade?"

"Norse blood, and Fair-truce doesn't hold for them."

Colum shook his head. "That's a question only the druids can answer. For my part I—"

He broke off, realizing that he was shouting. He took a deep, steadying breath to calm himself.

"Speak, then," he said. "Why did you rescue me? I owe you the courtesy of listening at least."

"You owe me the doing as well," Coinneach replied. "Unless the Faolta's word has become no more than the blustering of summer wind."

"I'm listening," Colum said, an edge returning to his voice.

"We're bound for Dairsean—the druids'

wood," Coinneach said. "There you will meet with Muman's champion to settle once and for all who will lead and who will follow."

Colum stared at him in shock. "Are you mad? You want me to fight Donnan while our enemies lie sleeping in Emain Macha, building their strength?" He turned to Fachtna, Muman's King. "Tell me it's not so."

Fachtna faced him, his hard gaze meeting Colum's incredulous stare.

"You fear to lose?" he asked.

"Fear to lose? You *are* all mad. You . . ."

Colum turned to look at the others in their small company and further words died stillborn in his throat. The men here . . . He was in the company of the Kings and champions of Aerin. Donnan and Fachtna of Muman; Coinneach; and Oran, the King of Connacht. Seanan, Connacht's champion; Aed, Kerry's King; and his champion, Broen.

"You pledged me your word, Colum," Coinneach said.

"I . . ." Colum slowly shook his head. "My word, yes. But my fight's not with Donnan. This dye"—he tugged at his hair—"and this guise . . . the need for them is gone. I can no more meet Donnan at the Fair now than I can walk into Fergus's Mi-Cuarta and ask him for his daughter's hand."

"You'll meet Donnan there," Coinneach

said, pointing ahead into the shadowed forest. "In Dairsean. Tonight."

"But—"

"Fight him and best him, and then together—with the united clans of Aerin beside us—we'll topple Fergus from the High King's Seat."

"It's madness," Colum replied.

But his decision was made. His features settled into grim lines and his gaze smoldered.

"Madness," he said again. "But you've my word in trust, so let us be done with it."

Coinneach nodded curtly and led the way once more.

NINE

Hooded men met them on the borders of Dairsean Wood. Without needing to be told, Colum knew they were druids. Who else would they be in this place? For Dairsean was a druid wood and—more important to their present undertaking—the one place in all of Uloth that would never know the footstep of Fergus or his Norse allies.

Only one of the hooded figures let his features be shown. Colum recognized him from the Mi-Cuarta in Emain Macha earlier that night: Ghabhann, the chief druid. He gave formal greetings to the Kings, then turned his attention to Colum and Donnan.

"You may take nothing into the wood," he said. "Not metal forged, nor bough of

tree, nor cloth woven, nor leather of beast, nor stone. Sky-clad the Goddess sent you forth; sky-clad you must meet this challenge."

Colum shrugged. Wordlessly he stripped.

"There is a glade," Ghabhann went on when both men stood naked. "North in the wood. You must circle it three times—nor let tree bough touch you, whether high or low, nor turn you aside for the same. The Goddess watches through our eyes; the Antlered God speaks through us.

"This is the first challenge. I will meet you in that glade to speak of the second.

"Now go!"

The druid's voice cut like a whip crack across the still night air. Colum paused for a moment, caught off guard, then he was running. But Donnan was already ahead of him, moving hard and fast. The big man ran like a hart and Colum marveled at the ease with which he dodged the tree boughs— here leaping one, there snaking under another that barely seemed to have enough room for a fox to squeeze under. He never touched one bough and, steadily, surely, he lengthened his lead.

Colum cursed. He could feel the eyes of the druids on him, standing hidden in the dark wood on all sides, marking each bough that slapped him, each one he failed to see. His bare legs smarted and stung. More than once he'd had to roll under a low bough

through patches of nettles. He bled from a hundred tiny thorn punctures. His breath came in ragged gasps.

He wasn't used to this—not freshly arrived from the Grey Isles as he was, where he was a captain of horse troops, not infantry. He was making a poor showing, and this was only the first challenge.

He reached the glade finally and began his circle. Donnan was no longer in sight. Except for his own breathing and the slap of his feet on the ground, Colum didn't hear a sound.

He went more slowly now, marking the obstacles, thinking it better to go slowly, than make a worse showing of it by striking every second branch that presented itself to his bruised limbs. On his second turn of the glade, he caught a flash of naked skin between the trees on its far side, and knew Donnan was winning. He put on more speed. Dodging the boughs, low and high, was becoming easier now, but it was still no use.

Pain stitched his side by the time he completed his third circle and ran into the glade. Sweat beaded his brow, falling into his eyes. It stung the host of tiny cuts on his thighs and legs, arms and chest.

Ghabhann and Donnan were waiting for him.

The big man stood loose-limbed and relaxed, his breathing easy. But seeing the

scratches on him, Colum took some small satisfaction in knowing that his opponent hadn't escaped entirely unscathed himself.

Colum's gaze returned to Ghabhann.

How had the druid arrived here before them? He'd seen Donnan running ahead of him, but Ghabhann . . .

"As the Goddess has seen," the druid said, "the first challenge is Donnan's."

Hooded figures stepped from between the trees, moving as silent as sidhe. They carried spears that they dropped at Colum's and Donnan's feet.

"The way is uphill now," Ghabhann said. "You each have three spears and there are three targets between this glade and the next that is the heart of the wood.

"Go!"

This time Colum was prepared for the druid's abrupt signal. And throwing spears he understood.

He snatched up the spears and sprinted forward, weighing the weapons as he ran. The throwing spears were short—in the old Erse style—and perfectly balanced.

He was ahead of Donnan by a half dozen paces when he saw the first target—a flicker of white cloth in the starlight. He threw his first spear, pinning the cloth to the oak tree behind it with a dull thunk. Donnan's cast followed his like an echo.

Muman's champion drew abreast of Colum as they ran on. They raced uphill,

dodging low boughs and the great oaks that appeared to lunge out of the darkness at them. On all sides they could sense the silent presence of the druids—watching, measuring—and then the second target was at hand.

Colum and Donnan threw as one man. Their spears winged towards the second target, but a bough deflected Colum's cast so that his spear struck Donnan's. Both weapons fell short.

Now only one target remained.

Colum ran as he never had before. The pain in his side was like a fire—piercing and deep. Underfoot, the forest's mulch gave his naked feet poor grip. Still he gained a pace on Donnan. Then another. He could see the last target now—just a tiny speck of white, far ahead of him. He put on a new burst of speed and drew ahead a little more. And then, when barely within range, he cocked his arm and let fly.

His spear struck true and he raced on. He heard the thunk of Donnan's weapon. A moment later, the big man was beside him and drawing ahead once more.

The glade was very close now. Colum could *feel* the opening it made in the great wood. And old though the forest was, in this second glade he could sense something older still.

He pushed at his protesting muscles. His legs churned, his toes digging into the

mulch for purchase. Then he was abreast of Donnan once more.

They ran side by side. Just before they tore into the glade, Colum threw himself forward. He slipped on the dew-damp grass, skidded a half-dozen feet and tumbled into a roll. But he was on his feet almost before his back had touched the ground. Silently, he stood beside Donnan, trying to still the rapid hammering of his heartbeat, the quick heaves of air that he needed to draw in.

As he looked around himself, he saw the source of that feeling of age he had sensed earlier. A dolmen rose grey and tall into the night sky—an old longstone, a finger of the earth pointing Lugh-high. And standing beside it . . . was Ghabhann.

Now how . . . ? Colum thought.

"The second contest is Colum's," the chief druid said. "The Goddess has seen."

The wolf grin returned to Colum's lips. He glanced at Donnan, but the big man only shrugged and grinned back.

"Now let you two grapple, here beneath the sky that the Antlered God himself may see your struggle. Let one cry enough, or be struck senseless, and the third challenge is done.

"Let it begin!"

There was no more chance for Colum to catch his breath or to ease his cramped leg muscles. Donnan's hands were on him as soon as the druid cried, "Begin!"

Donnan was a powerful man—a bear, like Artor. And the wolf, who depended on his speed and guile, couldn't hope to prevail caught in his grip. He needed to be free, to strike, draw back, and strike again. But Donnan's fingers were like vises; the power behind his shoulders as potent as that of the oaks that ringed the glade. He stood over Colum, forcing him down. In a moment, they would fall. And when they did, Colum would be on the bottom, helplessly pinned and with the last of his breath knocked from him.

There was no sense fighting the man, strength for strength, Colum realized. So he got a grip on Donnan's powerful forearms and let himself fall. He curled up his legs and curved his back. When they landed, Colum heaved up with his legs, arcing Donnan over him. The champion of Muman lost his grip as he flew over Colum's head.

Colum scrambled to his feet. As Donnan rose, Colum balled a fist and struck. Once in the temple. Again in the side of his jaw. Then he danced back—away from the man's flailing arms. He wouldn't be caught twice in that bearlike grip.

Donnan shook his head to clear it. A growl rumbled low in his chest. This time when Colum came at him, he moved like a cat.

He caught Colum's fist as it flashed toward him, his big hand enclosing it, and

hauled Colum closer. A moment later, and he had engulfed Colum in another bear hug.

Colum struggled to free himself, but the strength he needed simply wasn't there. The foot race through the woods had left him spent—too many years in the saddle had left him unprepared for this contest. Not so Donnan. He had trained all year for this day. And the man was strong.

In desperation, Colum brought his forearms up behind Donnan's back and clapped his open hands against Donnan's ears. The big man cried out. Shaking his head, he smashed his brow against Colum's forehead.

Colum's head rang. Lights flashed against his eyelids. Donnan increased the pressure of his grip until Colum could feel his ribs giving way. A moment longer, and they would crack. He needed air. He was dizzy from the blow he'd taken to his head and his ears still rang, dots dancing in his eyes.

Donnan increased the pressure again. Colum groaned, and then the red mist came spilling up to cloud his sight. Snarling, he struck Donnan's ears again, bringing to play all the force he could muster. The grip on his chest gave a touch. Colum struck him again, twisting his head to dodge the brow that came smashing towards him once more. This time it caught him only a glancing blow. The third time he struck the big man's ears, Donnan let him fall.

The battle-mist overcame Colum now. His knee lifted to drive into Donnan's crotch. As the man bent over in pain, Colum struck him a savage blow across the back of his neck with a closed fist. Donnan dropped like a felled ox and lay still.

But Colum wasn't done with him yet. Still cursing, he leapt on the fallen man. He grabbed a fistful of red hair and raised Donnan's head, meaning to pound it into the ground.

It was Fergus he saw lying under him. This was no contest of champions. It was a blood-feud between the Ard-righ and himself—a feud that could only end in one or the other's death. It could only end with the spilling of blood.

"Stop."

The word lashed Colum, piercing the red mists that bound his mind. He lifted his head and saw, not Ghabhann standing there, but another. A tall manshape from whose brow twelve-tined antlers sprung. The eyes that fixed their gaze on Colum were ageless, deep and knowing. Silently they spoke to him.

Would you break Fair-truce, Colum, Donal's son, and so be outlawed in truth?

The mist cleared from Colum's gaze—quickly and suddenly, like the long grass of Kerry's plains parting before a storm wind. He realized whose head it was that he meant to batter against the ground. Gently,

he laid it down. When he looked to the dolmen again, the antlered man was gone. He saw the chief druid regarding him with a curious expression in his eyes.

"Yours is the third challenge," Ghabhann said. "So the contest is yours."

Colum nodded in slow agreement. But still he regarded the druid. Still he knelt above Donnan, remembering . . .

"What is it, Donal's son?" the druid asked.

Colum shook his head. "I saw . . . another standing in your place. The Antlered One himself, I thought. . . . But that couldn't be."

"And why not?" Ghabhann asked. "On this contest rested the fate of Aerin's High Seat. Such is a weighty matter, worthy of interest to the Lord of Death and Rebirth, wouldn't you think? Do we not speak here of the death of one Ard-righ and the rise of another to his Seat?"

"It *was* him, then, that I saw?"

The druid shrugged. "Perhaps."

"And is it such a common thing for you that you can shrug it off so easily?"

"Common? No. But his presence is always in this place—his and that of the Goddess who rules even him. Did you not feel it when you entered the wood—and especially when you entered this glade? The age of this place, and yet the agelessness of it? He is wild, our Antlered Huntsman, and this

is an untamed place that is sacred to himself and the Goddess."

Colum shook his head again. "I don't know about such things."

Wearily, he rose to his feet.

"Donnan," he asked. "Will he . . . ?"

"Live?" The druid nodded. "We will tend to him. Go to your companions now. There are deeds that still need doing on this night and the dawn draws near."

Colum straightened his back.

"I will do what needs to be done," he said.

Turning, he began to retrace his way back through the wood, his thoughts on Meave again, and on his son. On Fergus and the struggle against him that still lay ahead. But as he walked, his mind filled with visions of stags and stag-browed men, of wolves and ravens, and of a woman from whose eyes the light of the moon shone.

The waiting Kings and champions of Aerin watched him step out from the wood and then pause. He said nothing for a long moment; he merely stood there under the trees—silent, dark-browed, eyes smoldering and fey. Not until Coinneach approached and threw a cloak around his bruised shoulders did he stir.

"I've fulfilled my side of the bargain," Colum said, "and in doing so, we have lost a strong warrior. So what now, Coinneach? Will you give me leave to do what *I* must

do, or have you more madness in store for me?"

Coinneach gripped Colum's hand. His face was grim, too, but in that grip was the thanks for which he had no words. Then he turned to the others.

"Well, brothers?" he asked the Kings.

"We will follow you," Fachtna replied.

"Then this is what we do tonight," Coinneach said as he turned back to Colum. "Tonight we go to spill a not-King from the High Seat of Aerin and cleanse these shores once and for all of Wodan's curs."

Colum nodded. He ached in places he hadn't even known he had muscles, but he allowed no sign of it to show in his features. He had waited too long for this moment to allow his body's weakness to rob him of his part in the King-breaking.

"Let me dress," he said. "And give me a sword."

<u>TEN</u>

"Fergus knows" was the news that waited for them when they returned to Emain Macha.

With still an hour or so until the dawn, the darkness in the eastern skies was already lightening with a wash of grey. An owl dipped mothlike above them, wings silent in the dark air. More than one man marked it as a harbinger of doom.

"He knows?" Coinneach said to the man who gave them his news. "How can he know? Who's betrayed us?"

The gathered Kings and champions of Aerin moved closer to hear the reply. They fingered the hilts of their axes and swords, dark Erse gazes turned speculatively to-

wards the twin towers that oversaw the Ard-righ's rath.

Flann mac Cu Uladh, the captain of Coinneach's who had come to them with the news, was more than a little ill at ease in the presence of such select company.

"It was no man of ours," he assured Coinneach. "But Fergus has Norse druids. It seems their *sight*'s as keen as that of our own."

Coinneach nodded grimly.

"We've lost the element of surprise, brothers," he said, turning to his companions. "So the stakes are no longer the same. Are you still with me?"

"We gave you our word," Fachtna replied.

"And the Fair-truce?" Colum asked.

Coinneach spat on the ground at his feet. "Fergus will break it—and then we will break him."

"There's more," Flann said, his discomfort growing at the tide of bad news he was forced to bring his lord. "Not an hour past there were two new prisoners brought into the Stronghold of the Hostages. One was you own druid Somhairle—"

"Somhairle?" Colum cried. "But that's—"

Coinneach put his hand on the Wolf's shoulder. His eyes went flat and hard.

"And the other?" he asked his captain.

"A boy," Flann replied. "I've heard it said

that it's the Ard-righ's own grandson—the one that was fostered to the sidhe."

There were times when Colum cursed the red mist that came over him in battle—the berserker rage that fed false strength to his limbs and sent him charging at his enemy, bare-fisted if need be and without a care for his own safety. But at this news, with the weariness of his ordeal in Dairsean Wood still on him, he welcomed it as he might a dear friend.

There among the Kings and champions, he drew his sword. He viewed the world as though through bloody gauze. Shaking off Coinneach's restraining grip, he set off to finish the business he'd left undone seven years ago.

Fergus had stolen all that was dear to him—Meave, their son, his friend. But that was only one side of the coin. The other was, could he keep them?

"Colum!" Coinneach roared. "Will you throw it all away?"

Colum turned. His sword lifted until its point was at Coinneach's throat.

"Will you stop me?" he asked.

Coinneach retreated a step. There was something new in Colum's wolf-mask of a face tonight. The red mist clouded his eyes—that was plain enough—but this time he seemed to have a tight rein upon it, a control that made it appear all the more fey and deadly.

"Won't you ever listen to reason without first arguing?" Coinneach demanded.

"I'm done listening to Kings. I ask you again: Will you stop me?"

"Lord ... ?" Seanan, Connacht's champion, began, stepping forward.

Coinneach waved him back.

"Let him go," he said. Then to Colum he added, "Listen to me, Donal's son. There will be no room in Aerin for a man who can't heed his King's word."

Colum met Coinneach's gaze, but saw in the King's features only Meave and Myrddin, and the features of a son whose face he had never known.

"Then there will be no home in Aerin for me," he said.

Turning, he strode away into the darkness.

Coinneach watched him go. His companions gathered silently around him, waiting on his word. When it came, his voice cracked the air like a whip.

"Gather the clans!" he cried.

Colum stopped long enough to don his mail and gather up three throwing spears before he marched to the High King's Mi-Cuarta. When he finally stood on its courtyard, his mind was empty of all concerns except for his cold rage. His anger deepened still further—spinning against the

Charles de Lint

borders of madness—at what he found
waiting for him.

Guttering torches cast weird shadows
across the courtyard, throwing their light
upon a terrible sight. As was the custom
with the Norse, when offering an enemy to
their thunder god Wodan, they had nailed
a man to an X-shaped cross.

This wasn't the first time that Colum had
looked upon such a sight. But every other
time it had been a stranger he'd found mis-
treated as was this man. This time . . .

They had bound Myrddin's mouth open
with a part of his staff thrust between his
jaws so that he could speak no spell. His
fingers were broken so that they could not
conjure. His head hung against his chest.
Blood dripped from around the nails hammered into his hands and feet.

He lifted his head as Colum stepped into
the courtyard. His eyes opened and in the
flicker light of the torches and the growing
dawn glimmer that spread from the east,
his pained gaze found Colum's.

"Dogs!" Colum roared.

The door of the Mi-Cuarta crashed open
and the Norse poured out. They formed a
line two-deep in front of the great wooden
building and locked shields. From the left
and right sides of the High King's rath,
more of the yellow-haired warriors appeared. Then Fergus stepped into the doorway. He leaned on a spear and regarded

88

Colum with as much alarm as a man might a gnat. Guttorm came out to stand at his side, dwarfing the Ard-righ with his bulk, a mocking grin on his lips.

But Colum didn't see them. He had eyes only for the crucified man, nailed to the wooden beams behind the double-ranked Norse. Myrddin's gaze held his like a vise.

A spear, Colum thought he heard Myrddin say, the druid's voice echoing strangely in his head. *Cast it straight and true into my heart, Wolf.*

Colum shook his head.

He couldn't do it. Not while there still remained the smallest measure of hope that he could rescue Myrddin and cut him down. Until he was dead himself, he refused to give up that hope.

Cast your spear!

The druid's voice hammered in between Colum's temples. Colum shook his head again and then Fergus was speaking.

"This is a King-breaking?" the Ard-righ asked.

His voice was thin in the near-dawn air, filled with humor. He hooked thumbs in his belt and smiled down at Colum.

"One man?" he went on. "This is a sorry army that Coinneach fields."

"Not one man!" Coinneach cried from the shadows behind Colum.

They stepped forward then and arrayed themselves behind the last man of the

Faolta clan—the Kings, champions and warriors of Legan and Muman, Connacht and Kerry. There were even men from the clans of Uloth joined with them—the same clans from which Fergus took his Gailana. Though they were raising swords against friends and kindred, they could no longer stand aside.

"You disappoint me, Coinneach," Fergus said. "I thought you wiser than this. We outnumber you."

It was true. There were at least two Norse for each man Coinneach had with him, and Fergus also had the Norse druids and his Gailana. Taking in the odds, Colum could only despair.

The Erse still disdained mail and shields, though their enemies had no such qualms. There was no room here for chariot work. It was man to man, and the Norse had the advantage. What use were spears and blades when the wall of locked shields would deflect them? The Erse would break on the Norse's ordered ranks like unarmed children falling under the blades of seasoned fighters.

He watched through the red mist that clouded his sight as more and more Norse arrayed themselves in front of the Mi-Cuarta. At a directive from their captains, they began to circle around to enclose the Erse clans. Then Myrddin's gaze called him

and whether he wanted to or not, he had to turn to look at the druid again.

Your spear, Wolf, Myrddin's eyes demanded of him. *Have you forsworn your trust in me as well? Cast your spear!*

Colum shivered and again broke eye contact. He looked to Fergus. His hand tightened on his spear's haft, but when the first spear was thrown, it left the High King's hand, not Colum's.

Colum dodged the cast. Behind him, a man fell, the High King's spear sprouting from his chest like an extra limb. Erse blood soaked Aerin's soil.

The Fair-truce was broken.

Something keened on the wind as the speared man died. It was like a wolf's howl, or the cry of the Antlered Lord's Hunt. A banshee's wail. The earth shook with a tremor as she accepted the lifeblood of one of her children. Colum imagined the sidhe shivering in their burrowed duns. Brigit loosing her daughter's ravens into the sky. Lugh turning his gaze away as clouds rose up to cloak the dawn.

A kind of understanding dawned on Colum then—born of the fey powers that rode the air, rather than reason. He cocked his arm and threw his spear.

Fergus leapt behind Guttorm before he realized that he wasn't the target. The iron point of the weapon pierced Myrddin's

chest, searched for and found his druid's heart.

A low rumbling moan grumbled like approaching thunder.

The Norse druids cast spells that proved useless as the clouds above the rath took on the shape of an enormous antlered man's head. The spear sprang from Myrddin's chest. The wound closed by itself. Antlers sprouted from his brow. The bindings that tied the broken haft of his spear into his mouth fell away. He spat out the wood.

"Cousin!" he cried to the face-shaped clouds above. "Will you let the not-King continue to torment your people?"

His voice was no longer his own. It was deeper, unearthly in its fey timbre. Thunder rocked the sky in response—sharp explosive cracks that set bones rattling. The voice of a god, Colum thought, though what walked the sky tonight was a god of Aerin, not the Norse's thunder god.

"I am the Green Man!" Myrddin replied.

Colum cocked his arm again, only this time it wasn't his own will that set his limbs to action. Another used him—the thunder in the sky, or that familiar stranger who hung crucified on the Norse's cross-beamed god offering. All he could do was watch the weapon fly, arrow-straight. It pierced the breast of the not-King Fergus mac Coemgen—Meave's father who had caused Col-

um's father to die—and pinned him to the wall of his own Mi-Cuarta.

As though that spear cast had been a lightning bolt, a new peal of thunder roared across the sky. The cross to which Myrddin was nailed grew leafed boughs. The nails popped loose and spat across the courtyard, but the druid didn't fall. The cross had become a giant oak and one great branch lowered him to the ground.

Colum shuddered to see what Myrddin had become. The antlers on his brow lifted like the branches of a thorn tree, high above his head. He wore a cloak of green leaves. His feet were hooves, his limbs gnarled like the roots of some ancient tree. He turned to the Norse druids. Lifting a hand, magefire blossomed in his palms and leapt out at them. The druids ignited like bundles of dry twigs and were consumed.

"Guttorm," the Green Man said in a voice that was more Myrddin's now than a stranger's. "Is there still a place for you in these isles?"

Struck dumb, the Norseman could only shake his head.

"Then be gone from our shores."

Guttorm's men looked to him for guidance. Their hands were no longer on their weapons. Their shield wall was broken, shields hanging at their sides in slack grips. Preternatural fears clouded the burly Norseman's eyes. He gazed from the ashen

remains of his druids, to his fearful men, to the weird being that faced him—antler-browed, more tree than man, with the magefire still crackling in his palms.

For a moment it seemed as though he would cast aside his weapons. His own fingers were slack around the handle of his axe. But then, with a hoarse curse, he swung up his weapon and charged.

Magefire leapt from the Green Man's hands to strike him, consuming him as it had his druids. And then, as Guttorm died, the semblance of the Green Man fell away from Myrddin and the druid pitched forward in his own shape to lie as still as death on the packed dirt of the courtyard.

For the passing of a few breaths, an utter and profound silence descended on the men in the courtyard of the Mi-Cuarta. Then chaos erupted as the two armies clashed.

ELEVEN

"They fought without heart," a Kerryman said.

"It's just as well," his comrade replied, "or there'd be still more of our own people lying here among the slain. As it is . . ."

The Kerryman nodded wearily. "Fergus is dead, but it's still a sorry day."

Colum was only half listening to them as he searched through the corpses near the entrance to the Mi-Cuarta, looking for Myrddin's body, but he heard that last comment clearly.

It was truly a sorry day, he agreed. They'd broken the High King, but the price had been dear. Too many lay dead.

Then he found the druid and all further

thought fled his mind, for Myrddin was still alive.

Colum handled Myrddin as though he was a baby, working him free from the press of the dead and carrying him to the doorway where there was a clear space. There, under the dead gaze of Fergus who still hung impaled from the wall of his rath, Colum bathed Myrddin's face and carefully looked him over. There were scars on his hands and feet, another over his heart where his chest showed through his torn robe, but no other sign of his terrible wounds. Even his fingers had been healed.

Myrddin's eyelids fluttered as Colum sat back on his heels.

"Wolf?" the druid murmured.

"I'm here."

"I was . . . mistaken."

"Rest now. There'll be time enough for talk later."

Myrddin ignored him. He sat up slowly, then leaned against the wall, spent by that small effort.

"When two men fight," he said, "and they're both Kings . . . What can there be but war?"

"It's over now."

The druid nodded wearily. "Over," he repeated softly. "You know, Wolf, the bards used to call me the Green Man and I . . . I always thought it a blasphemy of sorts. But

now . . . What lies within each one of us, do you suppose?"

"Our hearts," Colum said. "And our wills. The need to be free."

"Wild as the Antlered Man who walks the woods . . . in his eyes, the deadly beauty of a serpent . . . I *was* him, Wolf, for that moment, that flicker in time's shroud. I wonder . . . is he in me still?"

Colum was troubled to hear Myrddin speak like this. Myrddin, the druid. Who always gave advice. Who knew in the fall of scattered bones the days to come. Who could read the stars for portents. Who could ride the winds with his mind.

Had the god's touch on him stolen that sharp wit from him?

"Siochain," the druid said. His voice was suddenly stronger, not so fey. "I promised to bring you peace. Have you seen your son yet, Wolf?"

"I . . ."

Colum's mail was caked with the blood of his foemen and the many small wounds he'd taken in the battle. He was so tired that he could barely stand. His every muscle ached. Yet if one, or all, of these dead Norse were to rise, he knew he could find the strength to fight them all over again. But this simple thing of which Myrddin spoke . . . to go to Meave and his son . . .

That seemed beyond his present strength or courage.

Seven years was a long time. A woman might wait that long in a harper's ballad—but in this world? Wouldn't her eyes say as he approached: Why did you come now? Why did you not come sooner?

What had been done tonight—wouldn't it have been easier done seven years ago and so saved her the trials that she had suffered in between? What would he say to her when her eyes asked him these questions?

Myrddin's lips shaped a weak smile.

"Has the Wolf grown so timid?" he asked.

Colum shook his head. He drew a breath and started to rise, but then—

She was there.

There was no Erse sea, nor Nial's Arm, between them. No army of Norse, nor her father's Gailana. Only the space of three strides.

The morning sun caught her auburn hair and made it sing. She held the hand of a six-year-old boy whose features bore so striking a resemblance to his own that he knew it could only be his son. There was no reproach in her eyes—only a glittering light.

"I knew you would come," she said, as though they were, indeed, characters in some harper's ballad.

Slowly, wonderingly, Colum stood. He was as tongue-tied as a boy going to court his first maid at a Feis. But the words that were caught in his throat spoke through his shining eyes, until finally he found his voice.

"I would have come sooner—"

"Whisht," she said.

Then she was in his arms, ignoring the mail he wore and the blood of their foes that was upon it, seeing only the youth she'd loved, grown to be a man.

Young Connal regarded his parents for a long moment, then grew bored as their embrace lingered on, so he knelt down beside the druid. His small hand reached out to touch Myrddin's brow.

"They told me you had antlers," he said seriously. "Like Cernunnos himself."

"You can only see them in a certain light," Myrddin explained. "They are hidden things, it would appear. So well hidden that I never saw them myself."

"Is that my father?" Connal asked, pointing at Colum.

Before Myrddin could reply, Colum had turned. He lifted the boy and held him out at arm's length to look at him.

"I am, indeed," he said.

"They said you were gone."

Colum nodded. "But now I've come back, to make amends for the lost years, and I won't be leaving you again."

He held the boy close, snuggled into the crook of one arm while the other hugged Meave close to his side, and that was how they were found by Coinneach mac Conan, Ard-righ of Aerin.

"Colum," the Ard-righ said. "We had words, you and I, and now I wish they could be taken back. They were spoken in anger...."

"Though no less true for that. I can't stay, Coinneach. I'm done with the work of Kings."

"But where will you go?"

Colum looked at Meave. In her eyes he saw that she too was remembering a time seven years past when a young maid and her outlawed lover had spoken of the lands that lay across Atlanta where it was said the meaning of the word "King" was forgotten and no man or woman stood above the other.

"To Aerin Nua," Colum said.

"Is there no argument I could raise that would change your mind?"

"None."

Coinneach sighed. "I can't stop you. But if you should ever wish to return, there will be a welcome waiting here for you."

Colum nodded.

"We love this land," Meave added, "but it holds too many bitter memories for us. Perhaps someday—if the power those memories hold over us fades—we'll come back."

Her gaze traveled to where her father's body was impaled upon the wall of his Mi-Cuarta. She looked away, pressing closer against Colum's side.

"But I don't think it's very likely," she said.

"Go, then," Coinneach said. "With a King's thanks, and a friend's blessing."

TWELVE

They stood together on the shore, the Wolf and the Fox, the captain waiting at the ship's rail behind them for the word to raise anchor and be gone.

"You won't come?" Colum asked for what he knew would be the last time.

Myrddin shook his head. "But we'll meet again. Look for me when I'm least expected. There's work for me still in these isles—though not war-work, for which I give you thanks. When it's done . . . who knows where I'll wander?"

"You'll give my greetings to the Bear?"

"I'll drown his anger in a barrel of ale."

Myrddin paused, looking as though he had more to say, but then he simply sighed.

"Fare you well, Colum mac Donal," he said.

Colum clasped the druid to his chest.

"Farewell, Fox. Have a care with those spells of yours."

"It's apprentices that I've been warned against," Myrddin said.

Colum began to ask him what he meant, then thought better of it. Often Myrddin's explanations were more confusing than the initial question. At least the druid was back to his own self once more—speaking in riddles.

He gripped Myrddin's shoulder, then turned and made for the ship where Meave and their son were waiting for him, standing at the rail with their ship's captain.

Long after the anchor was raised and the ship rowed out to deeper waters where her sails were unfurled, Myrddin stood there by the sea, watching until the ship was just a speck, and then there was only the sea with no sail at all upon its horizon.

"At last you have your peace, Colum," he said.

He thought he heard the fey murmur of sidhe voices. He cocked his head to listen more closely, then shrugged. He wondered what shape the people of the Middle Kingdom would take in that new world to which Colum sailed. They would be secrets still, he was sure. Little mysteries.

Finally, as the afternoon leaked away and the night drew close, he turned and left. All that remained then was the sound of the sea, lapping against the shore, and the unseen presence of the sidhe, looking westward.

In time, they too were gone, and only the sea moved in the glimmering twilight.

THE BEST IN FANTASY

☐ 53954-0   SPIRAL OF FIRE by Deborah Turner Harris $3.95
   53955-9   Canada $4.95

☐ 53401-8   NEMESIS by Louise Cooper (U.S. only) $3.95

☐ 53382-8   SHADOW GAMES by Glen Cook $3.95
   53381-X   Canada $4.95

☐ 53815-5   CASTING FORTUNE by John M. Ford $3.95
   53826-1   Canada $4.95

☐ 53351-8   HART'S HOPE by Orson Scott Card $3.95
   53352-6   Canada $4.95

☐ 53397-6   MIRAGE by Louise Cooper (U.S. only) $3.95

☐ 53671-1   THE DOOR INTO FIRE by Diane Duane $2.95
   53672-X   Canada $3.50

☐ 54902-3   A GATHERING OF GARGOYLES by Meredith Ann Pierce $2.95
   54903-1   Canada $3.50

☐ 55614-3   JINIAN STAR-EYE by Sheri S. Tepper $2.95
   55615-1   Canada $3.75

Buy them at your local bookstore or use this handy coupon:
Clip and mail this page with your order.

Publishers Book and Audio Mailing Service
P.O. Box 120159, Staten Island, NY 10312-0004

Please send me the book(s) I have checked above. I am enclosing $_____
(please add $1.25 for the first book, and $.25 for each additional book to
cover postage and handling. Send check or money order only—no CODs.)

Name _____

Address _____

City _____ State/Zip _____

Please allow six weeks for delivery. Prices subject to change without notice.

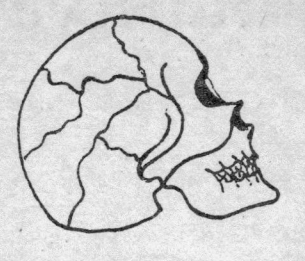

THE FINEST IN SHORT HORROR STORIES